A PROPOSITION OF SUBMISSION

EM BROWN

CHAPTER 1

Adeline Herwood gave a lot of advice that Deana listened to then disregarded. But on this night, as Deana sat at her favorite card table in her friend's private gaming club, she wished she'd listened to her mother and stopped coming here. Because standing at the threshold of the card room was Halsten Rockwell, looking as gorgeous as when she'd last seen him a year ago. Dressed in a perfectly tailored suit, he must've arrived from some important engagement. He entered with that quiet command, vaguely aloof, that she'd first attributed to arrogance. If he knew that he turned heads, he showed no evidence of it, at ease with the attention of others.

Heart hammering, Deana busied herself with collecting the cards at her table. How sharply her body had reacted to his presence, every nerve leaping to attention, as if their one-night stand had been only yesterday. She prayed he wouldn't notice her, though for weeks after their brief liaison she'd looked for him every night at the club. How often she'd recalled that night her body had thrilled beneath his hands. How often she'd lain awake taut and in need of release, yearning for his touch. She wasn't in love with Rockwell—well, maybe a little—but he'd ignited a flame that couldn't be easily quelled. Though she couldn't imagine any other man could have the same effect on her, and hadn't, she'd concluded that it was best to put him from her mind. If she were fortunate, she'd never have to see him again.

But, as usual, Lady Luck proved a fickle friend.

Deana shuffled the cards. Once. Twice. Three times. Like a rabbit alert to a predator approaching, she heard a friend of Rockwell come to greet him and indulged a small sigh of relief. The clock had struck midnight a few minutes ago, and the crowd at the club hadn't thinned. In her unassuming olive-colored blouse and jeans, she could've blended into the walls. Even if he noticed her, he wasn't likely to approach. He hadn't sought her out since their one-night stand. It was clear he was done with her and wasn't interested in renewing their acquaintance.

"You gonna shuffle all night?" one of the patrons at her table asked.

With a practiced hand, she swiftly dealt everyone at the table their cards, then poured herself a glass of wine as she stole a glance in Rockwell's direction. He'd taken a seat at the dice table, his back to her, though she easily recognized his lean and tall form, accentuated by the tight and exquisite cut of his coat. Brianna Walpole, a sexy frequenter of the club, sat beside him, fluttering her thick eyelashes. Deana finished off her wine in one swift intake.

But it was silly of her to feel the slightest hint of jealousy when she had no claims on him. That a woman of her modest situation had ever attracted the attentions of Halsten Rockwell was an anomaly. Gentlemen billionaires didn't date nearly-broke part-time art teachers/gaming club racketeers.

"Not another collector," her mother had groaned for the fifth or sixth time in the last months, that morning. They had cancelled their cable subscription over six months ago, but the company was still after the hundred or so dollars they owed for the last month.

Deana poured herself another glass of wine before collecting the cards. One of the men at the table stood up in exasperation after his loss, followed by another. She contemplated retiring for the evening but had won three hands in a row. A few more hands and she might make this month's mortgage payment. "Deana."

She looked up from the cards and into a pair of intense brown eyes under trim dark brows. How could he be more good looking than she remembered?

Calmed in part by the wine she'd consumed, she greeted him in a civil and even tone, "Rockwell."

Turning her gaze from his face—in particular those lips that had so forcefully and lushly taken hers once upon a time—she resumed shuffling the cards. To her dismay, he took one of the seats recently vacated, across from her. Brianna took the other chair beside him.

"Poker," Brianna pouted, her rosy lips pursed together. "My least favorite game. Take pity and help a girl out?"

He acknowledged the request with a slight inclination of his head, and Deana suspected he was honoring the *first* part of Brianna's request. Deana had little time to triumph over her earlier jealousy as he turned his gaze next on her. He held her stare briefly, but in those seconds, her heart beat in her ears. She couldn't tell if he was pleased to see her, though would he have sat at her table if he disdained her? Did he seek her company? He'd done so once before but in such an indistinct manner that she would never have known his intent except for his scandalous offer to her.

I'd have you in my bed, Deana. For one night, I'll take my pleasure of you, after which, your debt to me will be paid.

Her hands began to shake in recollection of that fateful loss to him. She finished shuffling the cards and took another drink from her glass.

"It's a hundred dollars to play," she said.

3

The ante was nothing to Rockwell, whose business holdings were extensive and international.

Brianna tossed out the appropriate chip and turned her large eyes on Rockwell. "You're good luck for me. Stick around."

Deana would've been more than relieved to have Rockwell leave with Brianna in tow. His presence made it difficult to concentrate, and as she'd discovered before, she needed her wits about her with this man. She dealt everyone their cards then stole a cursory glance at him. It proved a poor move since she found herself in his stare.

"Bet or fold?" she asked when she'd found her breath, silently admonishing herself for letting him unsettle her so. She doubted that she had an equal and similar effect upon him. In fact, he might have easily forgotten their liaison altogether. His last and only communication with her had been a short note accompanied by the gift of a porcelain elephant with ruby eyes. Despite being proud of her sensibleness, she'd kept the elephant like a sentimental teenager until circumstances had forced her to sell the treasure.

Watching as he put in two more chips without word or expression, Deana reminded herself to proceed cautiously with him. No doubt he'd played his share of this game, and she wouldn't want to wind up in the same situation she'd found herself a year ago.

Or would she?

She squirmed subtly in her seat, remembering the delicious ache between her legs, the burn of her ass where he'd landed his cat-o-nine tails. To quench the heat fanning through her body, she turned to Brianna.

"I can't remember, is a flush better than a straight?" Brianna asked of Rockwell.

"No," he replied.

Brianna knit her brows and bit her lower lip, which she

pursed and pouted as she stared at the cards. One of the other players sighed loudly.

"Halsten?" asked Brianna.

Deana waited patiently though she wished the woman would make a decision so that the game could be over. She intended to quit after just one hand and take her mother's advice with regards to the club—for the night at least. Despite her mother's disapproval, the club was their main source of income. She could make a lot more at high-stakes cards than she did as a part-time art teacher.

Brianna tossed her cards at the table. "I fold."

The next two players equaled Rockwell's bet. Deana looked at her own cards: all diamonds. Perhaps Lady Luck hadn't deserted her after all! A flush was a high note to end the evening on. She pretended to consider the matter then put in her two chips.

In the next round, Rockwell doubled his bet. The player beside Brianna folded, leaving three in the game. They went two more rounds before the third player folded. Deana eyed the pot. Despite her earlier dismay at Rockwell's arrival, she now appreciated that he'd sat at her table. She couldn't pass up that kind of money.

Déjà vu tugged at her. She'd sat across from him, a sizable pot between them, before. She'd had a strong hand then only to find herself indebted to him for five thousand dollars. A foolish desire to best a man who had all that she didn't—wealth, charisma, and model good looks—had persuaded her to bet more than she should have.

That wouldn't be the case tonight. She raised him another hundred.

As he contemplated his cards, she admired his classic features, his full lashes, the faint indent to the right of his mouth ... those strong, commanding lips.

Rockwell pushed his cards from him. "Your pot, Deana."

After inhaling in delight and relief, she collected her winnings with a calm that belied her fast-beating heart.

"You've done better," Brianna purred. "Shall we?"

Rockwell stood. "Take care."

Deana watched as Brianna took his arm. Their departure left her with mixed emotions. She couldn't deny her disappointment that he'd acknowledged her in only the most cursory of manners, though she couldn't expect the easy repartee they'd exchanged in private to take place in the club. She wondered if he would've been more friendly if they were alone? It was pointless to consider—she'd left thoughts of Halsten Rockwell in the past, where they belonged.

As she collected the cards, she realized they hadn't shown their hands. She turned over the cards Rockwell had held. Her eyes widened on seeing four of a kind, which would have beaten her flush.

———

What an odd man, Deana decided about Rockwell as she tugged on her coat. First, he'd gifted her the elephant, an antique she'd been able to pawn for a sizeable sum and had probably been worth at least twice what she got. Now he'd deliberately surrendered a winning hand. The wealthy could indulge in the strangest behavior, she supposed as she remembered his crazy wager that he would forfeit to her a thousand dollars if she failed to come at his hands. With that sum on the line, she would've thought it simple to withhold her orgasm. But her body had betrayed her better interests and surrendered to that sublime climax. Even now she couldn't contain the thrill from knowing that he could *not* have forgotten their night together or why else would he have deliberately lost to her? Did she dare hope that he was still interested in her?

She hurried down the stairs outside the club with a light and cheerful step. The late spring mist might soon turn into rain, and though her thin jacket would prove paltry against the cool night air, she was warmed by Rockwell's generous gesture.

But you've got to put him from your mind, said the voice of reason. *It was probably just one of those random acts of kindness. It doesn't have anything to do with you per se.*

"Yes, yes," she mumbled to herself, peeved that she couldn't allow herself even this small victory.

"Not taking a cab?"

She froze in her tracks. Deep in thought, she hadn't noticed the sound of footsteps behind her. Thank goodness it wasn't a mugger—or worse. She turned around to face Halsten Rockwell.

As if reading her mind, he said, "You're lucky I wasn't about to rob you—or worse."

In the dark she couldn't see his face well, but she heard the displeasure in his tone.

He continued, "Surely, after tonight's win ..."

She felt the weight of the money in her wallet, but she didn't need a lecture from the likes of him. "I like walking. This is one of my favorite routes."

Her assurance seemed to displease him more—she thought she saw his nostrils flare.

He narrowed his eyes. "Before or after three glasses of wine?"

It was her turn to be offended. She remembered his disapproval of her drinking, and though he made a good point, she didn't appreciate his unsolicited intervention.

"I'm quite capable of taking care of myself."

His frown conveyed the strength of his doubt.

"My car is ready and waiting ..."

She hesitated. It wasn't the ride but the thought of being in his company in close quarters that unsettled her.

"I'm not in the mood to be scolded, thank you very much."

His features relaxed and she thought she detected a smile

7

tugging the corner of his mouth. Once again, she had to force her gaze from those tantalizing lips.

"Nobody is," he murmured. "Especially when they deserve it."

She flushed at his words. Her ass smarted at the memory of how he had once doled out punishment.

"For your own sake, Deana ..."

She was sure the word he meant to use was *command*. Her spine stiffened. Their one-night stand was just that: one night. She was under no obligation to him. He was mistaken if he thought she'd play the good submissive at his whim.

But the effects of the wine she'd consumed lingered, and, in retrospect, she was fortunate that nothing tragic had happened to her the times she had walked home alone so that she could save money.

Cutting into her internal debate, he said, "I'd be grateful for the company." With an elegance that made her heart flutter, he offered his arm. She suddenly envied the likes of Brianna Walpole, who enjoyed his attentions.

With a fortifying breath, she took his arm, solid and strong. She was reminded of the many ways he'd once touched her, how he'd made her body burn with pain and pleasure all at once. Feeling her body begin to warm, she suppressed the memories as best she could.

They walked back to the club in relative silence. She considered a variety of comments, mostly about the weather, to keep her mind from wandering into the past and the attention away from the feel of him clasping her arm. Waving away his driver, he assisted her into the car. It was the same luxury SUV that had taken her to his home a year ago. Deciding to encourage her jealousy as a buffer to more tender emotions, she wondered how many other women the car had conveyed. Would Brianna Walpole be a passenger? Had she been a passenger?

When she looked across to Rockwell, his discerning stare made her feel as if her questions were written on her face.

"Why did you fold that hand?" she directed at him as the car drove onto the road.

Settling into the plush seat, he didn't deny her accusation. "Because I could."

"Is my situation that obvious?"

"It wasn't charity."

Taken aback, she couldn't voice her question: *Why else?*

Confused, she replied, "My prospects aren't *that* bleak."

"Sure. You're a regular just for sport."

She couldn't tell if he mocked her for amusement or to make a point. He sat away from the window, and his dry tone was too difficult to interpret. Whereas, apparently, he had no trouble reading her.

"I won't be a regular for long," she said.

"All that wine's a big expense."

Her cheeks grew hot. She almost retorted that she didn't drink much until he appeared. "And you're playing the Dom card with me, Mr. Rockwell." She emphasized the *Mr.* as, if her guess was right, a man like him wanted to be called *master* and not *mister.*

She thought she heard a smile in his response. "Somebody has to play the role."

She tried to tamp down her excitement: he remembered how long ago their last meeting had been, and he implied he wanted to be her Dom. Except that wasn't what he said, and she didn't need his kind of arrogant assumptions in her life. "So that's why you came back?" Brianna also worked at the club, as a professional submissive. She was building up a decent clientele, so Gabby had told her. That new venture of Gabby's was paying off, though it was risky.

Despite her light tone of voice, she wished she hadn't made that last comment. She'd thought herself better than that and was disappointed to find that she could be as jealous as the most petty of women.

9

She fumbled. "Gabby's happy with her."

"How are your mother and your aunt?"

"Better, thanks," she replied, relieved that the question saved her from further embarrassment. She would've asked after his family, but she knew his parents had passed.

Rain began pelting the car windows.

"And you?"

The gentle eagerness in his tone warmed her. They weren't lovers, but maybe they could be friends.

"I'm well enough now, I suppose … thanks to you."

He chuckled and stretched out his long legs.

Encouraged, she continued, "If you plan to make a habit of losing, we'll have to play more often."

"The club is no place for a young woman like you."

At twenty-seven, she didn't feel so young anymore, not when compared to, say, Brianna's twenty-two. "You're afraid I may wind up over my head?"

He shared in her laughter. "You may already be."

When the car pulled up in front of the house she shared with her mother and aunt, Deana felt disappointed they couldn't continue their talk.

Rockwell assisted her from the car. Taking the umbrella from the driver, he walked her to the door.

"Thanks … for the ride, I mean," she remarked as they reached the threshold.

"My pleasure," he said.

They stood too close beneath the umbrella for her to look long into his eyes. The rain served as walls penning them in, and despite the cool night air, she felt warmed by his nearness.

"I should return your winnings if you threw your hand." At his frown, she added, "At the very least, I should offer you the opportunity to win back your money."

"I'd rather have your company."

She stared at him, uncomprehending.

"I'm spending a few days in Napa at the Chateau Follet," he continued. "Join me?"

She hoped her mouth didn't fall open at yet another outrageous proposition from Halsten Rockwell. Gabby had told her about Chateau Follet, which had sounded like a private BDSM club.

"I take it you're not going just for the wine tasting," she said, unsure of how she should feel. Is that why he'd let her win tonight? Were her winnings intended as a *payment* of sorts for her company? Had he sought her out in coming to the club then? And above all, why her? Did she come across desperate to him? Easy?

"Look," she sighed. "I'm not interested in being your booty call."

She saw a muscle ripple along his jaw and decided it was best to end their conversation before she incurred his wrath.

"Good night."

She stepped out from under the umbrella and managed to unlock the door despite her trembling hands. Without a backward glance, she hurried inside the house, safe from the rain and safe from Halsten Rockwell.

CHAPTER 2

The Rain Persisted into the morning. Sitting in the comfort of his study, Halsten cursed to himself as he recalled the events of the prior night. He'd been too injudicious with Deana and had spoken with the hastiness of a teenager rather than the maturity of his thirty years. She had that effect on him. Despite the year that had passed, her influence only seemed to have grown more potent. Standing under the umbrella with her, their bodies so close it was miraculous that they didn't touch, he couldn't resist. He wanted another night with her.

No, he wanted more.

He rose from his chair to walk off the tightening in his groin whenever he recalled his tryst with Deana. How lovely her ass had looked quivering beneath the tails. How exquisite her form bent over the chair. How beguiling her groans as she succumbed to him. He'd had little doubt that she'd find pleasure in kinky play. He'd checked with her friend before making that initial proposition, but there had been no guarantees that Deana would take to submission. That she'd been so willing and so game for the wagers ... that had been rather unexpected. But it had been an unfair wager. He knew full well he'd make her orgasm.

What he hadn't expected was the impression their encounter had made on him. Though he hadn't anticipated they would spend more than one evening together, he had to stop himself from seeking her out in the following days. How often had he jerked his cock while on the chair to which he'd trussed her? Even now he felt a desire to venture into the room where he kept his BDSM implements and work his cock until he couldn't think any more.

He'd even gone to India in an effort to forget her. Granted, he had business in India to tend to, but the trip hadn't been necessary. He had no fondness for the long plane ride, and while in India, her absence was made more palpable. He found himself thinking of the temples that he'd show her and how delighted she would've been by the markets with their teas and silks. A visit to his favorite BDSM club in Mumbai proved as pointless in erasing Deana from his mind. Instead, it had sharpened his desire for her. Gradually, his business, a passing affair with the daughter of one of his parents' friends, and a trip to London with Lucille, his younger sister, did dim the memory of Deana. But when he heard a friend mention Gabby's club, he couldn't resist seeing if Deana still hung out there. He wondered if she'd kept the ivory elephant he'd given her in their last and only correspondence since their night together, but Deana wasn't a sentimental woman. He'd quickly gathered that her financial situation hadn't changed since they last met.

The ping of his cellphone interrupted his thoughts. It was a text from his sister.

Halsten scanned the contents of the long message. In between reprimands of his cruelty for leaving her with their Aunt Sophia and lamenting the boredom that would surely send her to an early grave, Lucille alternately scolded him and begged him to allow her to come back to San Francisco.

"Stop treating me like a child," she had complained on his last visit.

"Stop acting like one," he'd responded without lifting his eyes from the newspaper.

"I can't believe Mom and Dad made *you* my guardian!"

Shaking his head at the memory of her words, Halsten put away his phone. He knew he couldn't keep her from coming home. She'd finished the semester at boarding school, but he wanted her to stay away, since her main interest in coming home at the moment was a young man named Wilson. Lucy was too young to be getting serious with anyone. Distance and time would cool their interest.

If only the same could prove true for him and Deana.

T he winnings from last night's game with Halsten Rockwell remained in Deana's wallet. She hadn't wanted to touch them. She had no desire to keep his money, but her more frugal side wouldn't allow her to indulge her anger by tossing the winnings. Did he think that just because she had agreed to a one-night stand before—and only because she was under financial stress—that he could just waltz into the club and expect that she'd jump into his bed again?

But she was as indignant with herself, since a part of her *wanted* to accept his invitation. Still angry the following day, she went to the club despite her decision not to return for a while. She reasoned that another evening spent at the club meant avoiding her mother and aunt and their constant complaints. It had nothing at all to do with one patronizing billionaire.

He was not at all the reason she'd put on her best dress. The bright blue of the shift dress gave color to the dullness of her hair and plain brown eyes. Though she usually wore little makeup, she was more careful to draw attention to the few features she considered fine: her high cheekbones and unblemished complexion.

Her luck that evening proved unexceptional. She won a game then lost another. All the while she glanced at the entry of the card room, wondering if Rockwell would show up. The bottle of wine tempted her throughout the evening, but she was mindful of Rockwell's admonishment. She had no wish to provide him another opportunity to scold her.

She was in the midst of a game when Rockwell appeared. She fumbled her chips. Though Brianna was quick to approach him, he made no secret that the object of his gaze was *her*. He didn't look pleased. Deana wondered if she'd offended him. No doubt accustomed to women flattered by his invitations, he must've taken exception to her rejection of him.

"I think I'll quit for now," she informed the other players before taking her leave.

She went to the dining room to gather her thoughts. She couldn't hide from him all evening. What if he intended to come here often? That thought made her chest ache. What would she do then? She didn't want to go elsewhere. She'd simply have to find a way to ignore him, a task she knew to be easier said than done. Picking at the food on her plate, she wondered why she'd ordered a salad when she knew she had no appetite.

"You mind?"

As she was sitting, Halsten Rockwell seemed to tower over her. He was alone, with no Brianna Walpole in sight. He had a hand on the back of the chair opposite her, and she couldn't help but admire his long deft fingers. Those fingers had once fondled her most intimate parts in the most delicious way …

Snapping her attention away from his hand, she replied, "I'm nearly finished here."

He eyed the uneaten salad. Without a word, he took a seat at the small table. He ordered a Maker's Mark. She should've refused his request to join her. But her brain didn't function as well in his presence.

"I didn't mean to upset you. I'm sorry."

She blinked several times. Though she deserved his apology, she hadn't expected him to offer one.

"You should be," she answered, unsure of how to handle the surprise as she mindlessly moved the croutons about her salad.

"I just thought we might both enjoy a bit more time together, considering our last transaction."

She looked him square in the eyes. "That was a year ago. You think I've got nothing better to do than sit around waiting for you to hit on me?"

He bristled. "Of course not."

"So you say," she murmured.

His brows shot up, but then he met her grin. "Careful."

There was a salacious quality to his warning, and she decided further conversation wouldn't be in her best interests. She rose to her feet. "I accept your apology."

She extended her hand as an olive branch. He looked at it, took it in the warm grasp of his long fingers and held it longer than necessary. Her heart palpitated twice as fast.

"Friends."

She smiled faintly, then left the dining room as quick as she could. She doubted she could put two words together. She paused in a deserted hallway and forced herself to take a deep breath. Her cellphone buzzed with a text.

It was from her Aunt Lydia asking her to come home as Adeline had fainted.

CHAPTER 3

"**Y**our mother's okay. Her fainting might have been the result of consuming too much wine on an empty stomach, but we did do an electrocardiogram," the emergency room physician told Deana and Lydia. "Looks like she might have had a silent heart attack a few weeks ago."

"A silent heart attack?"

"A heart attack with no obvious symptoms. Did she complain about chest pain or show fatigue or trouble breathing?"

"She was taking a lot of Tums for her heartburn," Deana recalled.

"That can be a symptom of a heart attack. Has she been under a lot of stress in the last few days?"

"Nothing out of the ordinary," Deana replied. "She seemed well enough yesterday when I left. Aunt Lydia?"

Her aunt kept her gaze lowered. "We did receive a notice … just after you'd left, Deana. If the payments aren't received within a month, we'll lose the house."

"I thought we had an extension?"

Lydia shook her head. "One extension too many. We are

several months behind on payments. Something like twelve thousand dollars."

"Why didn't you tell me?"

"Your mother didn't want to worry you more."

Deana paled. The house was the only asset they had left. If they lost that, they would have nothing. And her father had purchased the house at a time when mortgage rates were relatively low. As a result, their monthly mortgage payments were less than what they would pay in rent.

"Reducing your mother's stress would undoubtedly help her overall health," the physician said.

Deana nodded. It would take an incredible streak of luck at the club to amass the amount needed. They'd long ago exhausted the kindness of family, mostly distant, and friends, which had grown fewer and fewer. She herself was already doing all she could, and there was nothing else to be done. Except … there was one man for whom twelve thousand dollars would be no hardship. Maybe Halsten Rockwell would help her, but how could she expect his generosity when she'd rebuffed him the other night? She doubted she had the courage to approach him. The thought of asking for his charity made her cringe inside. Pride won over pragmatism.

"What are we gonna do?" Lydia cried, wringing her hands, after the doctor had left.

"I'll think of something," she assured her aunt.

But she very much doubted her own lie.

———

Halsten leaned his head against the back of his chair in his office and closed his eyes. He didn't like the discomfort he felt. He should forget Deana—as he'd intended a year ago. She'd made it clear she wanted nothing beyond a platonic friendship with him. And it was just as well. He had his business and Lucy to focus on. He'd forget Deana once and for all this time.

"A Deana Herwood is here to see you," his secretary said over the desk speaker.

Halsten sat up. "Show her in."

He strode to the sideboard and poured himself a glass of whiskey. This was completely unexpected. Remembering how discreet she'd been with her first visit here in the dead of night, he wondered what could've brought her to see him now?

"Halsten."

He turned to see her standing at the threshold, as beautiful as ever, but for the quivering of her bottom lip. The thought of taking that mouth in his warmed his groin. He threw back the drink.

"Deana."

He noticed the tight manner in which she clutched her purse.

"Something to drink?" he asked.

Her mouth quirked to the side. "I thought you disapproved."

"Everything in moderation."

"I practice moderation, except when you're around, it seems."

She was mocking him. The imp. He suppressed a smile.

He gestured for her to take a seat. "To what do I owe this pleasure?"

Hesitating, she took a deep breath. Her bosom rose, and the image of her breasts trussed between his ropes flashed in his eye.

Still standing, she replied, "I came to talk about your invitation."

He wanted to close the distance between them and lift her face, which he'd cup between his hands, tilting her mouth up so that he could descend on it and cover it whole. Instead, he continued to stand next to the sideboard, patiently waiting for her to elaborate. He'd already apologized. Surely, she didn't come all this way to seek another?

"I'm maybe, possibly, interested, or open, to accepting the invitation to the Chateau Faux."

Her voice had lowered, but he'd strained and heard every word.

"Chateau Follet," he corrected.

"That is if the invitation's still open?"

Her obvious anxiety tugged at something in him. She still had a tight grasp on her purse.

"Sit."

She didn't move.

"Please, Deana," he added more gently.

She sat on the edge of a chair as if she might need to leap to her feet at any second. He sat across from her.

"The Chateau Follet is owned by Marguerite Follet. She hosts a lot of heavy players and just about anything goes at her chateau."

"Ah," was all she said, as if to indicate that that explained everything. "Are you trying to dissuade me?"

Hell no. He'd take her there now if he could.

"While there's hard-core activities at the Chateau, you don't need to do anything outside your limits. I want you to be completely aware of what you're agreeing to."

"Do any of these activities put me in danger or harm me in any way?"

"I'd ensure your safety."

"Then I guess I'm satisfied." The full weight of her gaze was on him, as if daring him to betray that trust. "But I have one condition," she continued. "You see, my situation—my family—I'm not going to beat around the bush: I need fifteen thousand dollars."

He sat in stunned silence, realizing she spoke with too much conviction to be joking. She was deliberately choosing to prostitute herself? He leaned back in his chair, giving himself a moment to process the situation. She wouldn't meet his gaze. He liked seeing her eyes. He could discern a lot through them.

"You're in need of money," he stated the obvious. He couldn't help but be disappointed that that was the motivation for her presence.

Her back stiffened. "Do you accept my offer?"

In a hot minute, the Dom in him responded. Instead, he asked, "What happened to the Indian elephant I gave you?"

She shifted in discomfort. "It bought us some time, but it's been a rough year."

The confession didn't surprise him, and he regretted his question as it clearly distressed her. He wondered how desperately she needed the money. If he were sincerely generous, he'd simply give her the amount she needed. There was a pitch of desperation in the way she spoke. But then he'd lose the opportunity to take her to Chateau Follet.

She must've interpreted his quiet as disinclination and said, "Is it … too much?"

"No," he replied. He would've easily agreed to her current proposition for more than fifteen thousand. No miser, he wasn't cavalier with his money except when it served a specific purpose or helped him achieve something he very much wanted.

And he wanted Deana Herwood.

He wanted her bent over a chair, tethered to the bedposts, or writhing beneath him. Only after he'd had his fill of her could he truly hope to release her hold on him. Feeling his cock stretch, he crossed one leg over the other.

"I'll need the money in advance," she stated evenly but in one breath.

He raised a brow. She was definitely desperate. "Time's a consideration?"

"Does that matter for you?"

Still wanting to understand the exact circumstances prompting her request, he contemplated whether or not to insult

her pride with further questions. "You trust me with your physical safety but not where it concerns your money?"

She reset her grip on the purse. If he could, he'd toss the
annoying article.

"I appeal to your kindness—"

The nobler part of him would have him give her the money
without condition. But he couldn't deny that the carnal part of
him wanted her beyond reason. What if this was his last chance
with her?

"What kind of trouble are you in?" he asked flatly. He knew
she kept to herself for the most part and respected that she wasn't
one to indulge in pity. If she was in danger, such knowledge
might influence his decision.

She had the impudence to let out an exasperated sigh. "*You*
had solicited me. I didn't realize that would include an inter-
rogation."

"Well, it's obvious my charm isn't the reason you're here."

This time she had the decency to blush.

"You underestimate yourself," she murmured.

She was playing at flattery. He had to suppress the rising
desire to reach over and manhandle her.

"So … do we have a deal?" she pressed.

"Look at me." Taken aback by his authoritative tone, she hesitated. "If you're going to come to Chateau Follet, you will obey
my commands. All of them."

He waited patiently for his statement to sink in. She met his
gaze. He drank in the sight of her. She was more lovely than she
seemed to know, with her intelligence, glowing face, and shapely
body.

"I would be a poor businessman if I advanced the whole
without collateral," he stated as he eyed her response carefully.

"Half then?"

He had one more test for her.

"Come here, and put down the damned purse."

Her eyes widened slightly. She was on her guard, but she did as told and went to stand before him. He appraised the length of her from his seat. Without warning, he grabbed her by the arm and pulled her onto his lap. His mouth covered hers. After a moment of surprise, her lips parted for him. He tasted her and delved his tongue into her warm wetness. When he felt a return pressure, he released her back onto her feet.

Noblesse oblige had never possessed the upper hand, and it was conquered for good by the kiss. The scent of her—a mixture of the lavender soap she used and the mint tea she drank—continued to linger in his nostrils, despite their distance. The blood was pumping in his veins, and especially his groin.

"So, you accept my proposition?"

"I do."

She emitted a small breath of relief. "When do I get the first half?"

"If you leave your bank info with my secretary, I'll have it wired today. We can leave tomorrow"

She nodded and picked up her purse. He was satisfied to see that she was a little flustered. Signing the agreement with flourish, he held it out to her.

"I'll take care of everything, you just pack an overnight bag … and prepare yourself." He pressed the agreement into her hand. "You'll get the balance after three nights at the Chateau Follet."

They shook hands. "Thank you."

He rose. "I'll walk you—"

"I don't need an escort."

He watched as she walked to the door, his gaze falling to her ass. With effort, he pushed the thoughts of what he would do to with backside from his mind. For now. "Tomorrow then."

"Tomorrow."

He sat back down only after she'd departed. Her words hung in the air, ringing with promise. There had been no hint of dread in her tone and none in her kiss. That she didn't shrink at his touch had made up his mind. As he'd suspected but begun to doubt, she still wanted him. He hadn't asked the obvious question, in part because he had no wish to dissuade her from her proposition, but she could've simply asked him for a loan without any condition to go to Chateau Follet. It pleased him to think it was because she wanted to go with him.

With renewed energy, he looked to finishing his work so he could turn his mind to spending the next three days—and nights —at Chateau Follet.

CHAPTER 4

C ould *Halsten Rockwell have been more irritating?* Deana fumed as she walked away from his office, the ghost of his kiss still burning her lips. Why did he sit there impassive, as if he could care less if she accepted his invitation or not? Recalling the brief but forceful way his mouth had claimed hers, she imagined he couldn't have been entirely indifferent. A small surge of triumph lifted her heart. He had, most importantly, agreed to her proposition.

She wished the kiss had lasted longer. It'd been unexpected and equally jarring when he'd returned her to her feet, almost as if she were a fruit and he was merely assessing whether she'd spoiled. Maybe he wanted to check that he still liked her? But if he hadn't known, why invite her in the first place? She might've accepted him the first time. The kiss affirmed to her that she had and still desired him, more than she had desired anyone before. Bereft of his touch, her body felt out of sorts.

The Chateau Follet.

She shuddered with anticipation, a heady mix of giddiness and fear. She recalled the implements and fixtures in his secret room adjoining the living room of his penthouse. He'd only used the flogger on her. The intensity of the experience had shocked and amazed her. She would've done it again and again. But could she withstand more?

And who else would be a guest there? She would've asked him more about the Chateau if she hadn't been in such a hurry for him to accept her proposal. He'd certainly asked enough questions of her, as if he were conducting an inquisition. Was it merely his arrogant nature? It wouldn't be easy to spend three nights with him, as his submissive, she assumed. *You will obey my commands.*

The realization sank in that she'd be at his mercy in a place she'd never been before, among strangers, doing things she'd never thought she'd be doing. She'd been quick to place her trust in him because she required the money, but maybe that wasn't such a good idea? Still, he'd proven trustworthy on their one night together, and he'd passed Gabby's checks to become a patron of her club, so she had reason enough to trust him, to a point. Having arrived home, she let herself in and went upstairs to look in on her mother. Adeline lay in her bed asleep. She appeared pale and weak. Deana sighed, knowing she was a great disappointment to her mother, who had thought Deana's desire to study art in college was completely impractical because job prospects were limited. Turns out Adeline had been right. Maybe she had been selfish. Maybe she should have given up art. She couldn't even land a job as a public school art teacher because she didn't have teaching credentials.

Her aunt approached. "What are we going to do?"

"See a friend," Deana replied, "a, um, friend's dad A business guy who's done well, and I think my father once did him a favor, so he might, uh, help us out."

"Who is he?"

"He lives in Napa County. I've got an old college roommate who lives there. I'll crash with her while I pay a visit to this guy. You'll watch after mom, right?"

Lydia nodded, maybe accepting the lie easily since the truth might have depressed her. Deana turned quickly to avoid further questioning and headed into her own room. For the health of her mother and for their situation, she needed to follow through with her plan, though it made her queasy. She had to tolerate the queasiness, ignore the doubts, and deal with the consequences.

She pulled the suitcase from under her bed and began to pack for her trip to Chateau Follet.

Before heading to wine country, Rockwell wanted to have lunch in Marin Country first. Though the restaurant overlooking the bay was small, Deana and Rockwell had a private room all to themselves. They had dined on crab salad with orange and fennel and steak with black truffle sauce. It was easily the fanciest meal Deana had ever had.

While Rockwell stepped away after dessert had been served to take a business call, Deana eyed the tempting bottle of zinfandel, a local vintage, upon the table. Rockwell would surely scold her if she helped herself to another glass. Well, she intended to keep her wits about her at the Chateau Follet. She focused on the dessert instead. It was a bittersweet chocolate fondant with cardamom ice cream. She had never tasted anything like it. Before she knew it, she was down to the last bite before Rockwell returned.

"Glad you liked the dessert."

She looked up to see the tall form of Halsten Rockwell at the threshold. Having just spooned the last of the ice cream inter her mouth, she couldn't respond. She could only marvel at how rugged he looked, even in his casual polo and khakis. She swallowed the food. Maybe she'd need some wine after all.

He sat down and poured a little more wine into her glass.

· · ·

"I get to have more?" she couldn't resist.

"Just a little more," he replied.

She took up the glass. "Are you going to dictate everything I do, like the amount of wine I can consume?"

"Pretty much."

His answer startled her since she'd meant her question rhetorically. She recalled his statement about obeying commands.

Casually he crossed one leg over the other. Once again, he seemed to read her mind. "The rules at Chateau Follet are simple. Please me and you'll be rewarded. Fail to please me and you'll be punished."

She took a deep breath as his statements sank in. "And how would I please you?"

"By following my orders at all times."

"You expect me to be a twenty-four-seven submissive?" she squeaked out.

He offered her a reassuring smile. "I have only three simple rules I want you to observe at all times; first, you will not flirt with any of the other guests at the Chateau."

"Jealous much?"

His jaw tightened. "While we're at the Chateau, you're mine; fully, completely, utterly mine."

To her surprise, she felt comforted by his statement. "Fine. What are your other rules?"

"You won't have more than one drink per day without my permission."

She had no interest in becoming inebriated while at the strange and unknown Chateau, but she bristled at the rule all the same.

"And?" she prompted with a twinge of exasperation.

"Last, but most importantly, you'll let me know if, at any time, you feel disinclined to follow my orders."

"Ah, such as your second rule," she could not help snark.

Abruptly he leaned over and grasped her chin, pulling her to him. "I could ask much more … and get it."

She stared into his gaze. The air around them crackled with tension. She wanted him to kiss her again. He was so close it wouldn't require much for their lips to graze, but he let her go and sat back in his chair.

"Do you require all your subs to follow these three rules?" she asked, feeling a little petulant at not having been kissed.

Instead of going for his dessert, he took a slice of bread for himself. "The second is unique to your situation. The first one is obvious to a practiced submissive, and I always articulate the third rule. I'm going easy on you since this is your first visit to Chateau Follet."

"You are?" She wondered how many women he'd invited to the Chateau more than once, though the answer shouldn't matter to her at all.

"Some subs are told where and how to stand, what to say and whether they may or may not speak at all."

"And when to use the bathroom, too?"

Nonplussed, he spread butter on his bread before replying, "Sure."

She churned this bit of information in her head.

"They do not speak unless spoken to," he continued. "They are obedient and always respectful."

"Sounds a bit … much."

"Some find it liberating, to be freed to experience."

"To be treated like a child," she countered.

He chewed his food evenly as he contemplated her. She found herself mesmerized by the movement of his jaw. *Damn.* The man was arousing even in the most ordinary of movements.

Needing to distract herself, she asked, "Are you always a dominant?"

After finishing his wine, he met her gaze. "Yes."

Despite her elevated concern, a dark, visceral heat pooled in her loins. She found herself simultaneously drawn and repelled. Had it been any man other than Halsten Rockwell, she would've rethought this whole trip. She imagined him giving her permission to use the bathroom. How was it possible that could be provocative?

And yet it was.

"My interest in the practice of BDSM is purely sexual," he added. "I'm not interested in how subs conduct their lives outside of Chateau Follet."

She gave him a dubious look.

"I don't do this because I'm a control freak. In fact, I'm giving the subs what they want, how they want to be treated. In the end, it's all for their pleasure."

She was quick to pounce. "Is that what 'dominants' tell themselves to defend their actions?"

"Didn't I please you before?"

The heat swelled between her thighs. She reached for her glass of wine, though it was quite possible the alcohol would inflame her more. "It doesn't please me that you want to dictate whom I may flirt with or how much wine I can drink."

"You'll think differently in time."

She was taken aback by the confidence in his assertion. "So ... I'm to be punished for not following your rules, but I may object to your rules at any moment?"

"You are free to leave Chateau Follet at any time. I won't hold you hostage or compel you to endure anything beyond your hard limits. But I will make it hurt so good you'll beg me for more. So, are you willing to open yourself to new experiences and trust me to guide you through them?"

How was she to respond when he phrased it like that?

"I suppose," she agreed.

Too distracted by the tension swirling in her lower body, she couldn't recall the other questions she'd wanted to ask. She shifted in her seat. Would she be able to survive three nights at Chateau Follet? Though a dominant, he'd indicated that he wouldn't control her every action except for his three rules, but then why tell her all that he had? Was she too critical? Or could she, too, find the domination he had described liberating and ... pleasurable?

When she looked back at him, she found he'd stopped eating and was staring at her.

"Are you done with the appetizer?" he asked.

She considered pouring herself another glass of wine to both take advantage of her time before his rules took effect at the Chateau and to defy him, but she didn't indulge the childish impulse.

"I am, thank you," she answered. "It was delicious."

He rose from the table, and she assumed they'd be on their way to the Chateau, as foreign a place to her as India, only she never doubted her hope to visit the latter.

But instead of opening the door, he locked it. When he turned around, the molten look in his eyes made her heartbeat quicken in a matter of seconds. Every nerve in her body leaped to attention. She watched with acute anticipation as he sauntered back to the table. He wanted her. That was plain. That knowledge served as the headiest aphrodisiac.

With a broad brush of his arm, he swept the contents of the table to the floor. Plates, bowls and utensils clattered below. Wine spilled from the bottle. One of the glasses shattered. She stared with mouth agape and looked quickly to the door, expecting their server at any moment.

"The door is locked," he said.

She looked once more to the floor. Her heart drummed madly. Was he going to take her here, on the table?

"But you made a huge mess!"

Rockwell pulled her to her feet. Though dampness had already begun to form between her thighs, she attempted to put

31

some distance between their bodies and glanced once more at the door, but he didn't appear bothered in the least by the setting.

"Can't you wait until we're at the Chateau?" she pleaded in hushed tones as she kept an ear for the sound of footsteps approaching. She'd never had sex in a public place before.

"No," he growled as he leaned into her. "Neither one of us wants to wait."

She felt her entire body flush. "You're ... no, this isn't the time or place for—this is so not appropriate!"

He circled an arm around her waist. "So?"

His mouth seared where her neck and collar joined. She knew instantly she'd lose the battle. Desire flared in her groin. As he kissed her neck, her back arched into him.

She made one final attempt. Why should she give into him so easily?

"The server's going to wonder why the door is locked."

"Let him wonder," he replied as he worked his lips and tongue against the soft spot beneath her ear.

The sensation reverberated to her extremities. He lifted her onto the table as he continued his assault on her neck. She moaned. When his mouth finally covered hers, the defeat of her reservations was complete. She allowed herself to succumb to the full weight of his kiss, glorying in the masterful way his tongue danced with hers. Her body reacted as intensely as it had a year ago, maybe more. Desire, hot and strong, coursed through her veins. She returned his heady kiss, drinking in the heat and wetness of his mouth as if it were her last.

His hand pressed against the small of her back, and she could feel his desire long and hard against her hip. With his other hand, he caressed the whole of her back. She marveled at his touch. There wasn't a part of her body that didn't revel in the way he manhandled her. She kept her own motions to a minimum, sure that they'd only feel awkward and inexpert compared to his.

He pushed her down and covered her body with his.

"Ah!" she cried when his tongue grazed her inner ear.

She froze at the sound of her own voice. Someone might have heard.

"We … we should wait …" she began, feeling sheepish.

With his knee, he urged her legs apart. His hand reached for her skirt. She stopped his hand and said between heavy breaths, "I can't, not here." She couldn't trust herself to be quiet. Not with the havoc he could wreak on her.

Sitting back on his haunches, he contemplated her. She sat up and said more forcefully, "People will hear."

"Shhh," he hushed as if calming a baby. "Open your mouth."

As her impulse was to obey him, she did. He took the decorative scarf off her purse and tied it over her mouth. Her heart pounded between her ears. She'd never been gagged before, and though she trusted him, the thought of not being able to speak or cry for help was alarming. How was she going to tell him to stop? Bad enough the server might walk in on them, but what would the man make of the scarf tied around her mouth?

He must have read the panic in her eyes as he said, "You won't need the safe word, but you remember it?"

She nodded.

He ran a finger along the edge of the fabric above her lower lip. "You look sexy in a gag, Deana."

With her mouth forced open, she found it difficult to swallow. The glint in his eyes called to that desire low and hot in her belly.

"Lay back."

She complied. After all, she'd offered to go to the Chateau Follet with him and agreed to three nights of kink, but she hadn't expected the play to begin this early.

With a slow hand, he drew up her skirt. Instinctively, she pressed her thighs together when she felt the air on her legs. He eased a hand between her thighs and pushed one to the side. Her pulse raced. She closed her eyes at what was to come next. What a sight she must be!

He leaned over her as his hand slipped into her panties.

"Shit," he breathed on discovering the fair amount of wetness there and looked at her with a satisfied grin.

With a soft groan, she pleaded with her eyes to make this quick. But he stroked her with the back of his forefinger with maddening slowness, gently nudging her clit with his knuckle. She wanted him to stop, pay the bill and escape this restaurant that she hoped she'd never have to see again. She didn't think she could look the server in the eye, knowing what she'd done on one of the tables.

She could push Rockwell away but the beautiful sensations fanning through her body stopped her. He circled her clitoris, wet and slippery from her juices. Her toes curled inside her sandals. Pushing all thoughts of the restaurant from her mind, she concentrated on that familiar and welcome ascent. She gasped when he slipped a finger into her pussy. He slid the digit in and out, making her pant.

Her mouth felt dry against the scarf, but she wanted to come. At his hands. On this table. He slid a second finger into her, and her muscles grasped at him, greedy for more of him to be inside of her. At last he quickened his motions. She gripped the table and writhed under him; her movement stifled by his weight. Tremors shot down her legs. She was nearing climax.

He eased his pace. Her eyes flew open. *God, no.* He wouldn't stop now? She arched her hip into his hand.

"You want to come, Deana?"

She nodded quickly.

He resumed his divine ministrations. She groaned every time his thumb struck her clit. It was as if a day and not a year had passed. He still knew how to touch her, knew her most sensitive spots. The tension inside her mounted. She squeezed her eyes shut against the impending onslaught. When he twisted his fingers and stroked the small anterior area of her cunt, she came undone, her spasms rocking the wooden table.

Her gag muffled her cries, though she couldn't be sure how effectively. The world swayed around her, and she had to close her eyes to calm herself. Only when her breathing had slowed to a normal pace and she'd returned from where he'd catapulted her did she open her eyes. She was met immediately with a gleam in his. She saw that he still had a bulge in his pants. He'd want his turn.

He offered her a hand and pulled her up, then untied the scarf and unwound it from her mouth. Next, he held out his handkerchief, a monogrammed finery. She gazed at it quizzically.

He leaned in toward her ear and explained huskily, "You're still wet, Deana."

She flushed to the roots of her hair and took the handkerchief, hesitating as she held the silk fabric. A fine rag for an indelicate task. Under his watchful eye, she pressed the handkerchief to her inner thigh. After she was done, she smoothed her skirt over her legs. He took the handkerchief from her and returned it to his pocket. Then he smoothed his shirt. His restraint contrasted sharply with the impatience he'd shown earlier when he'd cleared the table and lain her across it.

Crouching to the floor, she attempted to clean the mess and replace the items onto the table.

"Least we can do is clean the mess," she explained when he turned to look at her.

He knelt to assist her. Oddly, she relished sharing the task with him.

"I still can't believe you did this," she said. "Who knows, you might get banned from this place."

He smiled at her. "Good thing I own the restaurant then."

CHAPTER 5

Halsten remained silent as they drove to the Chateau. He hadn't meant anything to happen at the restaurant, but the scent of Deana, her longing look, undid him. Deana, too, was quiet. He hoped it was only that she was somewhat nervous and not regretting their arrangement.

They soon arrived at the Chateau. The structure had three stories with two pointed towers serving as bookends of the perfectly symmetrical façade. The steep hip roofs of zinc contrasted with the ivory stones. One would've thought the Chateau was plucked straight from the French countryside. It stood nestled among mighty oak trees and low hills still green from a wetter than usual spring.

The driver opened the car door and Deana gazed in awe at the chateau.

"It's beautiful," she murmured.

He led her up the front steps and introduced her to his former assistant, Bhadra. She now worked for Madame Follet, but she'd agreed to watch over Deana, as this was her first visit.

"You're in good hands with Bhadra," he said and felt Deana's arm tense.

"I'll show you to your room," Bhadra said warmly with only a hint of accent.

Deana withdrew her arm from his and followed the other woman inside. Halsten watched the two women until they were out of sight. Some anxiety on Deana's part was to be expected, but she didn't lose her poise. Having observed her and knowing her history, he couldn't help but admire her quiet dignity in the face of life's challenges.

After instructing his driver, he went to pay his respects to the proprietress, Marguerite Follet. He was admitted into the library, where he found Marguerite sprawled on a settee in front of the fireplace, gently swaying a fan of ostrich plumes. At her feet sat a beautiful young brunette reading aloud from a book of Shakespeare sonnets. On seeing Halsten, Marguerite unfurled a slender arm. He crossed to her and pressed her hand to his lips.

"You've taken an interest in literature?" he asked, amused, for despite the vast quantity of books in the room, Marguerite had never been known to read any of them.

She waved a dismissive hand. "Penelope here has a *belle voix*. She could read from anything and make it sound lovely."

From the gleam in her eyes, he deduced Marguerite had other interests in Penelope beyond the young woman's exquisite voice. She smiled at Penelope, who closed her book and politely withdrew from the room.

"She's young," he remarked of Penelope.

Marguerite raised her finely shaped brows. "You think I'm too old for her?"

"You, Marguerite, could rival women half your years."

Appeased, she admitted, "Penelope is twenty years younger. A *jeune fille douce*."

"Had it with men?"

She sighed. "Not done but a trifle bored, though less now that you've arrived. Where have you been, Halsten? Has it been years

37

since you were last here? I thought maybe you got married or something. Some Pac Heights heiress."

"We weren't suited to each other."

"Then who have you here?"

"A newbie—"

Marguerite pursed her lips. "I had Blythe here not too long ago with a newbie. Fell in love and married the woman."

"That's definitely not my intention."

"Something against marriage?"

"Not really, but ..." He shrugged, as if it didn't matter. It was more that he hadn't found the woman for him.

"But you haven't given up on your Dom life?"

"I'm here, aren't I?"

"Bring your newbie to me so I can meet her when she's settled."

As he left the library behind him, he contemplated the unexpected news regarding Blythe, a notorious player. Blythe had a bit of a reckless streak, and Halsten doubted any woman could interest him for long. And while Halsten and Blythe may have shared a mutual interest in the Chateau Follet, they wouldn't share the same fate.

Deana didn't know what to expect on arriving at Chateau Follet, but she didn't imagine an inviting home. It was tastefully furnished, its staff polite, and there was no evidence that the most kinky activities occurred within its walls.

She studied the small slender woman, her long dark hair wound in a braid down her back. The woman had large almond shaped eyes, which she kept focused before her. Deana could tell nothing from her.

"This is your room," Bhadra said.

Deana stood stunned at the threshold. The room was breathtaking. A large bed of carved ebony filled most of the room. The linens and plush pillows of vibrant orange and deep red with gold detailing flamed the imagination and spoke to passion. A beautiful vanity of engraved wood and tortoiseshell with shiny brass handles, coupled with a painted chair, was equally exquisite. The armoire with its intricate floral design and bold colors was unlike any furniture she'd ever seen. An intricate jali surrounded the window, tapestries covered the walls, and above the fireplace stood a vase of peacock feathers and a large mirror framed with geometric motifs. She imagined she stood in a palace in India.

"Mr. Rockwell requested a bath be drawn," Bhadra said. "I'll be your assistant."

Deana ceased gaping at her surroundings and replied gently and a little awkwardly, "What?"

"Mr. Rockwell wants his guests to be well taken care of," Bhadra replied with understanding.

"This is my, er, first visit here."

"Yes."

Sensing Bhadra was anxious to execute her responsibilities, Deana shucked off her jacket.

Bhadra showed her into a large bathroom. A circular tub set by a window was filled with steaming, fragrant water. "Towels," Bhadra pointed to a heated towel rack. "And there's a robe behind the door. Your suitcase is on the luggage rack in the closet. Can I assist you in anything else?"

Deana shook her head. "Thanks."

"I'll be back in half an hour to check on you. Mr. Rockwell has a special outfit he'd like you to wear."

Deana nodded. So much for his whole "I don't control a submissive's every move" thing.

But the bath felt *wonderful*. She wouldn't have minded relaxing hours in the tub, with a soap that smelled of sandalwood and cinnamon. The bath was over all too soon once Bhadra knocked lightly on the door, but Deana felt incredibly refreshed. Her skin tingled from the cleansing. Bhadra offered a milky cream to use, the most luxurious moisturizer.

Bhadra then produced a loose blouse with short sleeves and a low neck that she topped over Deana's head. She had Deana step into a layer of petticoat, then wrapped a long strip of silk dyed from safflower about the waist before draping it over the shoulder. Deana marveled at the comfort of the sari.

She gave Deana a pair of beaded cloth slippers and waited while she slipped them on. Then, at the vanity, Bhadra braided her wet hair, coiled it on top of her head, and added a jasmine sprig.

"Do you require anything else?"

Deana stared at herself in the mirror, feeling out of place. It felt odd. Was it cultural appropriation to be wearing this? But the clothes were beautiful and comfortable. She considered asking Bhadra what she knew of the Chateau but decided not to keep her.

After Bhadra left, Deana ran her hands down her sari and admired the intricate weave of the fabric. She stood and looked once more around the room. It contained none of the implements that she'd expected—no whips, crops or sticks. A closer examination of the tapestries revealed elephants, tigers, a man playing a reed, a woman and a man …

She leaned in closer and saw a man and a woman in a tight embrace, her legs wrapped around the hips of the man. The images below all contained naked couples. One had the woman sitting on a prone man, facing away from him, his hands on her breasts. Another featured a woman bent in half, her hands on the ground, while the man stood behind her, gripping her waist. Deana felt warmth in her cheeks and a stirring in her groin.

"Depictions of the Kama Sutra."

Whirling around, she saw Rockwell standing at the door.

"Ah," was all she could think to say. "You've read it?"

He went to stand beside her before the tapestry. "I haven't studied it extensively, but I have read it in the original Sanskrit."

"Do you speak Hindi as well?"

"Yes."

Huh. A scholarly billionaire. He was unusual. He looked her over then turned her away from him, placing his hand between her shoulder blades. Her breath caught when his hand slid down the middle of her back to her waist. She hadn't thought her back to be so sensitive and *stimulating*.

"Lovely," he murmured.

She wished he'd caress her back again. But when he was still, she turned to look at him. His eyes were like dark pools of chocolate as he looked down at her. The corner of his mouth quirked upward. He slid his arm around her waist and pulled her to him.

Her heart drummed in anticipation as she was pressed into his hard body. She waited for him to kiss her … and waited. He wanted to kiss her. She could see it in his eyes. She could feel it in the erection against her stomach. Why didn't he kiss her?

He planted a soft and chaste kiss on her brow. "Sleep well, Deana. There will be long nights ahead."

Abruptly, he released her. She watched, bereft, as he waved his hand and left. When the door had closed behind him, she cursed. Why build her lust if he had no intention of resolving the tension? Was it his intention to build anticipation or merely to tease her to prove his power?

She'd have to take matters into her own hands. She crawled into the luxurious bed and pulled up her skirts underneath the covers. Finding her clit, she sighed and sank into the pillows. As she stroked herself, she wondered why she desired this exasperating man? He was hot, but she'd known good-looking men who hadn't affected her so.

Compared to her experience at the restaurant earlier today, her own fingers felt slight and unsatisfactory against her clit.

After a few minutes, she relented. She wanted him and him alone. She watched the simmering fire in the fireplace until she fell into a deep slumber with hopes that her patience would be rewarded tomorrow.

———

The brightness of the sun slipping through the curtains informed her that it was late in the morning. She stretched her arms above her. The night before, she had been too nervous to sleep well , but having spent one of the most comfortable nights, she felt rested and refreshed. She stared at the designs in the canopy above her. Her body surrounded by soft and sumptuous fabrics, she felt as if she'd woken in the chamber of a princess. With a contented sigh, she threw back the covers and walked over to the sideboard. Someone had left all the toiletries she needed. Just as she had finished cleansing her face, Bhadra entered with a tray. "Good morning."

"Good morning," Deana returned.

After setting the tray on a small table, Bhadra opened the curtains.

Drawn to the coffee she smelled, Deana sat down at the table and helped herself to the delicious meal of eggs, bacon and bread. Bhadra busied herself with laying out the clothes that she must've unpacked from the suitcase.

"My clothes will never feel as pleasant after having worn a sari," Deana remarked.

Bhadra gave her a small smile.

"You work here regularly?"

"Yes."

"Do most of the guests dress up?"

"Mister Rockwell requested it specially for you."

She was unsure if she should be pleased that he'd singled out the outfit for her. She decided to take advantage of the opportunity that Bhadra was less reserved than last night.

"Does he come here often?"

Bhadra paused. "It's been some time."

Deana mulled over the information. "Are there many other guests at the Chateau this weekend?"

"Not more than usual. Shall I do your hair?"

Deana went to sit at the vanity. Bhadra uncoiled her hair and removed it from its braid. As she brushed her hair, Deana considered which question she wanted to ask next and how to phrase it to get the best answer possible.

"You may return later, Bhadra."

Rockwell stood at the door. Dressed in a blue linen shirt and spotless white trousers, he presented a more relaxed version of himself. Bhadra nodded. "Yes, Mr. Rockwell."

He watched her leave—with some tenderness, Deana thought but couldn't tell with certainty. She remained seated at the vanity, not knowing what to do. She wasn't in her element here at Chateau Follet.

"You sleep well?" he asked as he strode over to her.

"Yes, thanks. Are you in the habit of entering a woman's room without knocking?"

He smiled a little but didn't answer her question. Instead he produced a large velvet box.

"To complete the ensemble," he explained and opened the box.

Deana gasped at the jewelry she saw. The little diamonds and rubies were laced together with gold in the most intricate and elaborate designs. He removed the necklace, set the box on the vanity, and went to stand behind her.

"I couldn't," she objected immediately.

"You will."

"I'd be afraid something terrible would happen to it."

"Are you defying me?"

He pushed her hair to one side and fastened the necklace

around her. It served almost like a collar, covering most of her neck. Little red beads dangled like raindrops from the bottom row of the necklace. Methodically, he attached the other pieces: earrings that dangled like miniature chandeliers from her ears; a bracelet that fit first like a ring about her middle finger and ran down the back of her hand before encircling the wrist; and a headdress laid down the center of her head and onto her forehead. Every time his fingers grazed her skin, she felt a rush. The weight of the jewelry, like an extension of his hand, continued to caress her. That familiar tension down below began to simmer.

Rockwell stepped back and looked at her reflection in the mirror. Deana stared at the same in awe.

"It's from one of the best jewelers in India," he said.

He traced the bottom of the necklace with his forefinger. She shivered as his finger glided along her collar, and suddenly the unquenched desire of the prior night flared through her. She didn't want to be denied again.

"What is your wish today?" she asked.

A muscle tensed along his jaw. "I thought I'd show you the extensive grounds. I'll have Bhadra prepare a picnic."

His answer disappointed her, though at any other time she would've delighted in a romantic picnic.

"Ah," she said flatly. Recalling how she'd once seduced him, she taunted, "Is the Dom a gentleman today?"

He raised his brows, though he seemed pleased. "Patience is a required virtue."

She refrained from pouting like Brianna Walpole, but her desire wouldn't be ignored. She squirmed in her seat. "I had expected there to be more, er, action here."

He cupped her chin and turned her gaze to his. "You have much to learn, Deana."

"Then begin your lessons—"

"I have."

"—and, please, don't prolong them. I'm an avid student." She fixed her most smoldering stare on him. "Don't you have an appetite or are you needing resolve?"

She dropped her gaze to his crotch. It was risky challenging his manhood, but she had no interest in a picnic before her lust was relieved.

He didn't take the bait. "I don't need enticement to ravish you."

"Then ravish me." It was the boldest statement she'd ever made. "Teach me," she urged when he didn't respond.

He gave her a serious stare. "You're short on patience, but it can be forced on you."

She didn't understand his statement, and she didn't care. At last they were going to play, or better still, he'd attend to the heat in her and satisfy it.

"Tell me, Deana, did you pleasure yourself last night?" Stunned by the frankness of his question, she had no reply. "I won't repeat myself."

The sternness in his voice prompted her to speak. "Pleasure myself?" She felt herself blushing to the roots of her hair.

"There's no shame in it."

"I know, but why do you ask?"

"I'd like to witness it."

Her eyes widened. Maybe she preferred the picnic after all. "I forgot, Bhadra could return at any moment."

"She won't."

She hesitated, then remembered a year ago, when he'd had her do the same with him in front of a mirror. Was that his kink? She shifted. He folded his arms. "Now, Deana."

"I should remove the jewelry," she said. "They're too precious to risk damage."

"They're fine."

Having run out of excuses, she blurted, "So this isn't going to be about my pleasure after all?"

His face was impassive. "Your pleasure ... through mine."

His words shot straight to her pussy. Indignation and desire fought for dominance in her, making her silent and immobile. She'd been a fool to think she was ready to submit to the likes of Halsten Rockwell.

"Deana, don't make me punish you on the very first day."

CHAPTER 6

Halsten saw both fear and anticipation in her eyes at his statement. He knew when he'd left her room last night that he'd left her wanting. It hadn't been easy. He had wanted to make her come as she had on the table at the restaurant, but she needed to be well rested. And a slight delay of gratification could heighten her eagerness.

His own pants had been fit to burst last night. Even now, as he looked at her in those bright hues and sparkling jewels, her one arm completely bare, he had to strengthen his own patience. He reminded himself that he had far more years of experience in BDSM than she did, had learned from a practiced teacher, and been here before.

But he didn't think he'd judged her wrong. Her passion was apparent, and she was no stranger to BDSM. He understood that her responsibilities and the weight of uncertainty made the opportunity for abandon appealing to her. She could appreciate releasing control, in the right circumstances, to another.

When she made no move, he rolled his sleeves up his arms.

"Let's begin."

He pulled her to him by the arm, startling the breath from her. To encase her to him, he circled his other arm around her waist. As he gazed down at her, he shook his head at himself. Did he really think he could resist her? It'd been hard enough before, but he'd made the task twice as hard by having her dress like the goddess she was. Her earlier flush of indignation contributed to her appeal. Desire glistened in her eyes.

Leaning down, he caressed the part of her neck below her ear with his mouth. He felt her relax against him. When he trailed kisses down the side of her neck, a soft sigh escaped her lips. He shifted his hand on her lower back to position her better between his legs. Her body felt perfect pressed to him. The blood heated and churned in his groin.

He moved his mouth down below the necklace. She arched her back, causing her hips to move into him. He put his hand to the back of her head to hold it still when he took her wet and waiting mouth. The freshness of her bath from last night coupled with a nondescript scent all her own made for a heady mix that made the blood pound between his ears and in his cock. Parting her lips with his, he tasted of her. Deeper and deeper his tongue went. Her breath hitched at the penetration. His mouth moved over hers in a constant, forceful motion. He allowed her little chance to return the kiss, a statement as to who held control. She could only submit to his plunder.

His hand traveled up her back, gently groping between her shoulder blades before finding and removing the pin that held the pallu in place. The fabric slid off her shoulder. With a swift and practiced hand, he unwrapped the rest of the sari. The garment fell to the ground with ease. This was how he wanted her, naked and willing. He dropped to his knees and grasped both her hips, pulling her to him and drinking in the sight of her bared midriff. She let out a shaky moan when he kissed her there and darted his tongue at her navel. He inhaled the musk of her desire.

His cock stretched even further. Reaching up, he grabbed a breast and kneaded the heavy orb. He brushed his thumb over her hardened nipple. Her head fell back, and she threaded a hand through his hair.

"Ask permission," he told her.

She looked at him with a dazed expression, her eyes glossy. "What?"

"No moving without permission."

He could see the thought sinking in. She withdrew her hand.

"Good," he murmured. "Obedience shall be rewarded."

She stiffened in obvious resistance to the idea. Undeterred, as he'd expected she wouldn't fully accept the practice—at least, not at first—he continued to work the nipple. Pinching, pulling, rolling it between his thumb and forefinger until she whimpered. He pulled the rest of the fabric off of her. Rising to his feet, he lifted the exposed breast and attended the nipple with his mouth. She groaned with every swirl of his tongue, every nibble, every suck. When he had her panting, knowing she was wet with desire, he turned her around and pushed her up against the nearest wall. Her cheek was pressed against a tapestry depicting Kama and Rati locked in a naked embrace.

"Your obedience shall be rewarded," he repeated, "and your defiance punished."

He stepped into her, pinning her body to the wall with his. He ground his desire against her.

"What is the safe word?" he demanded.

"*Rati,*" she answered quickly.

"Good."

He circled his right hand around her waist and between the front of her thighs, rubbing against her. She quickly dampened. He fondled her more and she writhed, her movements hampered by the wall and by him. Her legs shook a little.

His left hand went back to the same breast, mirroring the

rhythm of his right. She tried to push into his hand, her pussy wet and warm. "*Ohhhhh*," she moaned, a melodious sound.

When he sensed her nearing her peak, he slowed his ministrations. "I told you to pleasure yourself."

She shifted her weight but said nothing. He pulled his right hand away completely. She let out a sigh.

"I'm waiting."

She squirmed. "I ... don't want to."

"Consider yourself lucky that I didn't ask you to pleasure yourself in front of all the guests at the Chateau."

She sucked in her breath.

"Do as you're told." He seized her moment of indecision to step back and admire her body. He remembered well her full ass and how it had quivered under his flogger. He slid two fingers down the curve of one buttock, admiring its contour, before palming it. He returned his other hand between her thighs. She let out an immediate moan.

Grasping her hand, he forced her to join his caresses. She put up a short-lived resistance until desire overcame her resistance. Her hips swayed gently to their joint strokes. He pressed his erection against her ass and closed his eyes for a brief moment. With her body rubbing against him, her grunting and groaning filling his ears, it was all he could do not to unbutton his pants and release his cock.

And they'd barely begun.

He took a deep breath and gathered his concentration. As he kissed her behind her ear, a particularly sensitive spot for her, he gently retracted the hand that held hers. She didn't stop. Satisfied, he reached for her breast and kneaded the flesh while his fingers toyed with the nipple. He ground his hips into her backside, bumping and grinding her into the wall. Eyes shut, she masturbated herself more vigorously. His blood was on fire with the motions, the sounds, and the scent of her desire wafting into his nostrils, triggering something primeval and animalistic. Pinching her other nipple, he sent her over the edge. She cried out. Her body shook against him. He caught her around her waist and pinned her to the wall before she slid to the floor. Her breath was fast, her cheeks flushed. He kissed the tip of her ear.

"Well done, my pet," he commended. "Now, about your punishment ..."

D eana could barely hear him through the loud thudding of her heart. Overwhelmed by the intensity of what had just happened, she kept her forehead pressed to the wall and her eyes closed, not ready to face the world, still waiting for the currents in her body to run their course. She could hardly believe that she'd done what he'd asked. *But how amazing the results.* Once she'd begun, the titillation had surprised her. Eventually the needs of her body had consumed her. The feel of his hands on her body, the confined space between him and the wall, all added to the concentration of desire. If only he'd taken her and fucked her, the experience would've been perfect.

She felt feathery light kisses planted on her neck. His hand caressed her upper back, between the shoulders, before he backed away from her. Her nakedness came back to her, with the cool air now reaching her back. Feeling far too exposed before his discerning eye, she bent down to retrieve her clothes.

He stopped her. "We haven't finished yet."

Of course. He hadn't come yet. She was surprised he'd withheld as long as he had and wondered how he intended to finish.

"Go over to the foot of the bed," he instructed.

She did as told.

"Grasp the bedpost with both hands above your head."

Fulfilled but a moment ago, she felt a new warmth circulating in her. Her timidity had not completely dissolved, but she was feeling more at ease with his directions. Again, she did as he commanded.

"Don't let go. I could tie you to the post but prefer not to."

Would he take her from behind? Her pussy throbbed at the idea. She heard his footsteps and wondered what he was doing. The sound of leather slapping against wood made her look over. He had a riding crop in his hand.

"Your punishment—"

"But I did as you said," she protested.

"Not very promptly."

"But—"

"Are you arguing with me?"

She contemplated the tone of his voice. It would be worse for her if she argued.

"No," she relented, for now. She had fond memories of the time he took a flogger to her, but it'd been some time and had happened only once.

"Good."

She felt the crop caressing the contour of her rump.

"Lovely as ever," he murmured.

Even as she swallowed in fear, the wetness between her legs increased. She tightened her hold of the post. Would he exercise restraint, as this was her first visit to the Chateau? She'd only ever been spanked with a hand or a flogger before.

With the crop, he began tapping the bottom of one cheek. Gradually, he increased the amount of force to a tolerable sting. Then, unexpectedly, he whipped the crop against the other buttock. Deana sucked in her breath, mostly in surprise. It was a sharp but not overwhelming blow, the sensation more pinching than what she recalled of the flogger. Her cunt pulsed.

He flicked the crop at her with increased strength. This time she shut her eyes against the smarting. It felt as if someone had stuck a pin in her ass. She grasped the bedpost as if she could diffuse the pain into it. He let the crop fall several times with lighter, almost teasing, strikes. When she thought she'd acclimated to the punishment, he jolted her with a potent blow. She screamed and felt her eyes water.

"Need your safe word?"

She thought of answering *yes*, but pride mixed with curiosity won out.

"No."

He swatted her ass twice more. The area of her groin grew warm along with her ass. How could she be so excited while clinging to a bedpost, nude except for the jewelry that concealed nothing, submitting herself to being whipped with a crop meant for a horse? If she'd known she'd find herself in this position, would she have agreed to coming here?

The answering moisture of her arousal slid down her inner thigh. Rockwell caught the rivulet with the crop and slid it up along her leg until it skimmed her pussy. Her legs weakened with anticipation. He rubbed the crop against her flesh. She moaned low. The tip of the crop bumped against her clit. He retracted the crop and slapped it against her buttock, but this time she fully welcomed the touch, the pain fueling the hunger burning between her legs. Again, she felt the crop gliding across her slit, sliding with ease across her wetness.

O.M.G. First her hand, now a riding crop. She shivered but didn't resist the pleasure building inside her. She wanted the stimulation, wanted it harder and faster. And he seemed to know her body better than herself. He began rubbing her with the crop in earnest. The stinging of her ass hadn't receded and made her more alert to the wonderful sensations fanning from her groin. Needing to come more than anything, she grasped the bedpost and fucked the riding crop in return.

She came gloriously, her body engulfed in flames of desire. Pain mingled with pleasure to produce a sensational end. Her limbs shook. Barely able to hold onto the post, she was vaguely aware of her own cries. The thrusting of the crop slowed. Occasionally, the tip of it pushed against her clit, shaking quivers from her body. When the crop finally retracted from between her legs, she slithered to the floor. Eyes closed, breath fast, she would've preferred to fall into bed to recuperate but didn't have the strength.

After what felt like a long time, she pried open an eye and dared to gaze at Halsten Rockwell.

CHAPTER 7

D espite the molten look in his eyes, Rockwell showed no evidence of being affected by what they'd done. Deana's gaze fell to his crotch and the bulge there. Well, maybe not totally unaffected. She marveled at his poise. She didn't know a lot of men with restraint when it came to sex. Her lack of control over her own wayward body surprised her, and yet the self-indulgence provided a liberating feeling.

"That was, um ..." she began. She couldn't think of the right adjective to describe what she had just experienced.

He unrolled his sleeves. "Bhadra will see that you're ready for our picnic."

Deana found herself annoyed by his calm. It seemed unfair that she should be in such a state of discomposure, giving in to her physical needs, while he chose to proceed with a damn picnic. Why didn't he fuck her? Didn't he want to? Had she dissatisfied him in some way? She watched him return the crop to a cabinet, studying him for signs that he might be flustered in the slightest. Her body couldn't have asked for a more satisfying and exquisite conclusion, but she now felt vaguely unfulfilled.

Returning to her, he assisted her to her feet and kissed her lightly on her hand. A shiver went through her. The simplest touch from him had that effect on her.

"I'll be back in an hour," he informed her before walking towards the door. He paused at the threshold. A devilish glimmer flashed in his eyes. "You are overcoming your inhibitions. Be ready for more."

Her cheeks heated. With some relief she watched him leave. She had a lot to digest. The fresh air might help. And she looked forward to engaging in normal activities with Rockwell. Except, from his statement, he might make the normal into something kinky. She pulled on a robe and was picking up the sari just as Bhadra returned. Flushing, she covered herself and tied the robe shut.

"Some ointment," Bhadra said as if nothing were amiss.

Deana accepted the small container and set it on the vanity.

"You should apply it now. Do you need any assistance?"

Deana colored. How had Bhadra been prepared with the ointment? She wanted to ask Bhadra but was too mortified. In silence, she allowed Bhadra to remove the beautiful jewelry, which she placed carefully back in its case.

She excused herself to the bathroom and applied the ointment, which did soothe the marks on her ass. Somehow, though, rubbing them was titillating. She cleaned up and went back out. There was a pretty spring dress laid out on the bed. "Is that for me?"

"Yes, Mr. Rockwell picked it out. You don't have to wear it, but he thought you might enjoy it. He said he never paid you back for ruining a garment of yours."

She had thought he'd more than repaid her with the gift of the antique elephant. Still, as she fingered the dress, what would be the harm in wearing this pretty outfit? She hadn't had a new dress in a long time.

Deana looked at Bhadra. "Have you been acquainted with Mr. Rockwell long?"

"Some years."

"Have you always been at the Chateau Follet?"

"No."

She didn't want to pry by asking more questions, so she just nodded.

She thanked Bhadra and proceeded to get ready, anticipating the return of Rockwell.

Halsten grunted as he came. He shook his head and leaned back into the armchair. Not what he truly desired but at least the tension would be relieved for a time. Nothing less than her pussy would ultimately satisfy, and he'd been tempted from the moment he entered her room and saw her wrapped in the sensuous fabric of the sari. The jewelry had enhanced every part it touched—her brow, her neck, her ears, the top of her hand, her middle finger. If he dressed her again with the baubles, he'd kiss each spot before it became bejeweled. Of course, the jewelry looked most beguiling when she was naked. His cock twitched at the vision of her ass. The marks of the crop had adorned those full and sumptuous cheeks with as much beauty as the jewels did her neck and hands. But he'd withheld himself because he wanted the focus to be on her pleasure. His time would come soon enough.

Deana was as beautiful as he'd imagined she'd be in the dress he'd gotten her. It hugged her curves in a suggestive way without being obviously tight. She'd curled her hair, one coil resting against that sensitive spot on her collarbone.

He extended an arm. "Marguerite wanted to meet you."

The hostess was found lounging on her patio, eating grapes, like an image of Dionysius, a copy of *Vanity Fair* on her lap. Despite her years, Marguerite had a youthful glow, and her complexion seemed to have found the fountain of youth—or at least a very convincing serum.

"Welcome, my dear," she greeted Deana warmly. "I hope you found your first night comfortable?"

"I did, thank you," Deana replied. "Bhadra has been quite helpful and attentive."

Marguerite looked at Halsten. "She is a wonderful addition to the staff. How long do you intend to stay?"

"Three nights," Halsten replied.

"In the West Wing? Or do you plan to venture into the East?"

He could feel Deana's inquisitive gaze. "West."

Marguerite turned back to Deana. "My chateau is at your disposal. If there is anything you need, don't hesitate to ask. If I may be presumptuous, and I often am, you are in good hands, my dear."

He noticed the color intensify in Deana's cheeks and briefly wondered if he'd be able to keep his hands off of her during their excursion.

"Halsten told me you're headed out, so I won't keep you."

She waved them away and went back to her magazine.

As he escorted Deana out, he knew it would not take long for her to ask, "What is the East Wing?"

He eyed her carefully. "The activities in the East Wing are more … intense."

She regarded him with equal care. "How intense?"

If he were too explicit, he might frighten her. "The guests in the East Wing have been to Chateau Follet many times." She waited for more information, but he didn't provide it. "We'll keep to the West Wing," he assured her.

She looked at him squarely. "Have you been to the East Wing?"

He paused. "I have."

"Do you prefer it?"

"Depending on the company."

To his relief, she changed the subject. "Marguerite seems nice."

"Did you expect otherwise?"

"I had no specific expectations."

Outside, they walked across the lawn and onto a path. They ambled along, going toward a spot he knew would provide some of the privacy Deana seemed to prefer.

"Is she married?" Deana asked.

"She used to be. But, unless polygamy becomes legal, she has too many lovers now to consider marriage."

She turned her clear eyes on him, her gaze asking, "Are you one of them?"

"No."

He led her on, passing a few sculptures and a garden, then up a hill overlooking the property. They found a flat area above one of the hills and set up their picnic.

"It's beautiful here," she murmured as she looked out at Chateau Follet in the distance. The fresh air and minor breeze agreed with her.

After setting out the bread, cheeses, berries and chocolates, he poured two glasses of wine.

"Am I allowed?" she asked wryly.

"I'm not planning to ravish you here."

"Why not?"

Her forwardness took him aback. He handed her a glass of the wine to provide himself a second to recover. The pulse in his cock throbbed. "Are you trying to tempt me?"

She took a sip of the wine. "And if I were?"

He didn't expect but was certainly not displeased by her show of shamelessness, as it proved she felt more at ease with him.

"I don't have any reservation about baring your ass out here."

She quickly popped a truffle into her mouth, as if it could provide her a protective barrier. "Is this all part of your seduction?"

"You propositioned me," he reminded her.

"And you didn't require much seducing. Why?"

Her simply query was not an attempt to fish for compliments as someone like Brianna Walpole would've done. Deana seemed genuinely mystified. He watched as she nibbled on the food, waiting patiently for his answer.

"Or is it any willing woman would do for you?" she prompted.

"I sensed you had a spirit for adventure. Haven't we discussed this before?"

"And what did you see in me that would suggest I liked my ass whipped by an overbearing Dom?"

He grinned. There were many women he found more attractive the less they spoke, but he enjoyed talking with Deana. "It was a gamble. But it's paid off, hasn't it?"

She blushed. He liked the rosiness in her cheeks. Liked that it owed its appearance to him.

She lowered her gaze. "I've surprised myself. It's kind of … embarrassing."

He covered her hand with his, an instinctual move and not one he necessarily intended. "There's nothing to be embarrassed about."

She gazed at his hand on hers. "I'm not as experienced as you are."

Retracting his hand, he helped himself to the bread. "But you've shown strength and interest despite your inexperience."

"How did it start for you?"

Vivid images danced in his mind. Silhouettes of a man and a woman behind beaded curtains.

"A club in the city," he said. "Started by observing, and soon an older Domme began mentoring me. Her submissives and play partners seemed so happy. She'd learned to develop a sense of how her partners felt, and how to ask the right questions of them."

He eyed her carefully but saw no judgment in her reaction.

"So you do a lot of BDSM?" she asked.

"Not as much as you think," he replied.

"You're not a frequent guest of Marguerite Follet?"

"Bhadra didn't mention that it's been some time since I was here?"

She looked surprised that he knew about her conversation with Bhadra. Of course, he hadn't wasted a moment that first night before mining Bhadra for all the information she could offer on Deana.

"Did you know Bhadra through Chateau Follet?"

He could tell she wanted to know his relation to her. But he didn't mind her questions, though he usually had little patience for prying questions, even from Lucille, who usually had a great many.

"I brought her here," he replied. "I was traveling in Rajasthan, India with a friend when we came across the funeral pyre of Bhadra's father in the Deorala village. Her mother committed sati, though the practice is illegal. Unmarried, Bhadra had no one to support her. Our guide asked my friend and I if we could help. If you want to know more, it's Bhadra's story to tell."

"I've dreamed of going to India."

Appraising her, he stretched his long legs out before him and leaned back against his elbow. "A lot of women dream about finding Mr. Right or winning the lotto. You dream about traveling to India?"

"When I was small, my father had a client who spent time in India. He gifted me a small tapestry. It was of a little Indian girl beside a peacock and lagoon. I loved that picture."

"The reality of India can be harsher than your vision. It's a country with many facets."

"I don't doubt that. Our country has many facets, good and bad. But maybe things wouldn't be so harsh for some in India if you paid your employees there higher wages?"

"If we paid them higher wages, outsourcing wouldn't make as much financial sense."

"You'd be left with hiring Americans. What a dreadful thought."

His brows rose at her rare instance of sass, which he found kind of appealing, as it came with a flash in her eyes.

"What's more American than maximizing profit?" he returned. It wasn't what he believed, but he wanted to fan the flames in her eyes.

She folded her arms. "I see. Greed trumps duty to your fellow man."

He suppressed a grin. The blood in his groin had already warmed during the previous topic of how he got his start with BDSM. Now his cock was at stiff attention. "Come here."

CHAPTER 8

S till contemplating his directive, she made no move. Halsten could tell she was still annoyed with him.

"For what purpose?" she asked.

"The purpose doesn't matter," he replied. "I want you to come here."

"Can't bear a little criticism?"

He helped himself to the strawberries to improve his patience and resist reaching over the food and wine to manhandle her. "Not at all. But the issue isn't as simple as you think. My company is responsible to a lot of different stakeholders."

"Meaning those on Wall Street. Screw everyone else."

He had humored her detour long enough. "Were you a troublesome little girl? You seem unable to obey orders."

She, too, turned to the strawberries for distraction. "Yeah, there's this particularly bossy guy I know …"

"Dominant," he corrected. "And a few well-administered punishments should address your defiance."

She squirmed and picked the greenery off the tops of the strawberries. "If you like being the disciplinarian, why not find a full-time submissive to tyrannize?"

Overseeing Lucille was enough for the time being, but he kept that thought to himself. "Bossy, overbearing, tyranny. Anything else?"

"How much time do we have?" she threw back at him.

Reaching over, he grasped her wrist and pulled her to him. "What does it say about you, that you still crave and burn for my touch?"

He saw her breasts rise with extended breath. She blinked against his gaze, then pulled herself from his grip.

"I don't crave and burn for your touch." She acted as if she were offended.

He raised his brows, intrigued by the challenge. "Prove it."

———

Deana felt her mouth go dry despite the moist berry she'd stuffed in it. She should've known she was playing with fire when it came to this man. She didn't want to go near him, but if she didn't please him, he might call an end to their time at Chateau Follet and she'd lose the opportunity to earn the remainder of the funds she required. She hadn't been here a day and was now facing her second "punishment."

She considered renewing their debate about his business, but he wasn't likely to take the bait a second time. She suspected he'd only humored her the first time. The thought disturbed her. He could afford to humor her, as he could afford many things. She didn't often bemoan the difficulties in her life—her mother and aunt did enough of that for them all—but she couldn't ignore the inequity between her situation and that of Halsten Rockwell. Did he deserve his place in the world more than she? If she were in his place, she wouldn't indulge in tormenting people, or using them.

"If you won't take my word for it," she replied, "then that's the end of it."

"Hardly."

His impassiveness was maddening. She finished off her wine to indicate the picnic was at an end.

"I don't feel like proving anything to you."

"You don't want to be proven wrong."

"No. Just because you say 'jump', doesn't mean I have to ask 'how high?'"

"But that's what you essentially agreed to in coming here with me."

She didn't have a response. It wasn't like her to be so provoking. She'd encountered men far more difficult than him at the club, and in life, and so had no explanation for why Halsten Rockwell could incite her with ease.

Laying back, he crossed his hands behind his head. "I'm not going to reach over to get you. Just know that the longer I wait, the greater the punishment."

"What sort of ... punishment?"

"I've got a number of nice options to choose from, but I think the punishment should fit the crime."

She fidgeted with her now empty glass while stewing on his latest statement. It was becoming clear that she had few choices here at the Chateau—of her own devising. Maybe if she'd been more creative, she wouldn't have had to turn to Halsten Rockwell for help. Well, there was little to be gained from crying over spilt milk. She'd made her bed and should see it to its end.

Without word, she rose and resettled herself on his side of the picnic blanket. He turned to his side and fixed his gaze on her like a predator that had its prey cornered. Her pulse quickened.

"Satisfied?"

"Partly," he murmured. "Unbutton your dress."

Dread and a dash of excitement filled her. "Now? Out here? But we could be seen."

"We could."

He must've noticed her pale since he added, "Do you see anyone besides the birds in the trees?"

"Not *right now*."

"I hadn't thought to start your punishment out here, but there are branches easily within reach."

She bit back an oath and reached for the buttons, which she undid one by one with reluctance. Maybe someone would come along and prevent anything from happening. Surely, he wouldn't continue with someone else here?

"If anyone were to come," he said, "it would probably be a guest at Chateau Follet. And chances are they'll have witnessed much more than this."

She thought of the East Wing and wondered if the guests there would be fine with what they did. As was he. Of course, it was easier for him since she was the only one undressing.

The wicked gleam in his eyes made her heart pound. Under his intense stare, she slid her arms from the sleeves. She wouldn't do any more unless directed. He regarded her from the top down, and despite her discomfort, she felt herself growing warm in her groin. How could she be mortified and aroused at the same time?

He moved to sit behind her and brushed her curls off the back of her neck. Gently, he pressed his lips to the exposed area. Her skin tingled where he caressed. This wasn't good.

"Any more criticisms?" he invited as he continued to plant kisses about her nape.

Was he daring her to provoke him?

She steeled herself. "Would it just be a waste of time and energy? Or maybe it serves your vanity?"

"My vanity?"

"Yes. Narcissistic men like being the subject of conversation, good or bad."

"You think I'm a narcissist?"

"Why would you invite criticism?"

He put a hand on her rib cage to hold her still, as she'd been leaning away from his kisses. Amazingly, it didn't matter where he touched, her whole body was his instrument to play.

"Would it surprise you to know I'm interested in what you think?"

She hadn't considered that possibility. Her cheeks colored at the disservice she'd done to herself. No, not to herself. She was confident of her opinions. She'd maligned him without real thought or knowledge. Maybe she should rethink her views?

His hand moved to cup her breast. She quickly glanced around, but not even the birds in the trees could be seen. Again, no, she was safer being angry at him. She'd fought this battle before and lost. He'd wagered a thousand dollars that he could make her come at his hand. Now there was only pride at stake, lessening her odds further.

"Only a narcissist would need to prove himself," she said, squaring her shoulders.

He squeezed her breast in response. She felt the compression through her bra, and her back arched of its own accord, pushing her breast further into his hand. The nearness of his body, and his breath on her neck, threatened to send her thoughts scattering. He flicked his tongue against the back of her ear then slid his hand beneath her bra and pinched a nipple. She did her best not to whimper. They weren't in the privacy of his secret room. They were in plain, open view. That fact might provide defense against his advances.

Or not. As he rolled her hardening flesh between thumb and forefinger, she felt pulses shooting from her nipple to her pussy. What had happened to her anger?

"There's no shame in submitting to me," he whispered in her ear.

She shivered but did her best to resist. "Easy for you to say."

"Ah, but the rewards are shared. Lift your dress."

She gasped, "Please, I—"

This time he didn't wait for her to comply and reached for the hem himself. She stopped his hand.

"We aren't in the East Wing," she protested.

"No one is here watching."

"That could change," she snapped, angry that they were repeating an earlier exchange.

"Which makes it exciting," he growled.

She ground her teeth. *There was no winning with this man!*

"This doesn't prove anything," she asserted desperately.

"No more delays, Deana. Lift your skirt. If you truly don't want to, use your safeword."

At the severity of his tone, and not really wanting to stop, she decided to comply. She grasped the hem of her skirt and slowly inched it up her legs, exposing her thighs.

"Further," he commanded.

She pulled the dress to her pelvis and closed her eyes. Someone would come on them, surely, despite the fact that they were some ways from the Chateau.

"Further."

Why hadn't she worn underwear? The breeze tickled her exposed flesh.

"Now spread your legs."

Her mind clawed for an escape, but no argument would deter him this time, she knew. Slowly she widened the distance between her knees. What did he intend?

Holding her against him with one arm, he reached between her thighs with the other. His hand went beneath the dress, and it took all of her not to shut her thighs, even as she tingled in anticipation. When his fingers touched her flesh, she had to close her eyes, unable to watch, in case someone walked up. Her legs were bared and spread for all to see. At least the dress still covered part of her.

Gently, he fondled her clitoris. Her breath became ragged. She leaned against his shoulder for support. His fingers circled the little nub of flesh, encouraging it to swell. None of her past boyfriends had attended her needs with such skill. She admitted, to herself in particular, that she couldn't resist his touch.

And he'd prove it.

Her body grew warm despite the rise of a cool breeze. He quickened his strokes, driving all thoughts from her as the intensity of sensations overcame all else. He played with her swollen clit, teasing and torturing it, till she writhed and panted. The collection of wetness between her legs seeped into her dress, but she didn't care. Her body had begun its ascent. Only when she reached the top could she hope for blissful relief.

When his fingers slipped lower, she gasped. Her whole perineum lit up. Curious at the small area of immense sensitivity, he fondled it frequently, strumming the base of her clit to the edge of her opening. Each time she cried out uncontrollably, shuddering as bolts of lightning shot up her spine. She almost wanted him to stop, but he worked the area without mercy. Unable to withstand the powerful stimulation, she quickly came undone, crying out loud enough to send birds scattering from the trees as her body bucked against his. Even as her body went over the edge, he didn't stop his rubbing until he'd squeezed every last shudder and every last cry from her. Feeling as if she'd just been shot into the sky like a cannonball, she sagged against him without word or movement, hoping for recovery.

What had happened? The potency of what she'd just experienced both enlivened and frightened her. That her body was capable of such intense euphoria was a marvel, and part of her very much wanted an encore, but such loss of control, such helplessness at his hands, surely didn't bode well for her careful life. She didn't need feelings awakened that would only have to be denied.

"Damn," he breathed.

Rockwell seemed equally amazed. He brushed a stray hair from her eyes and kissed her on her brow.

"You're not gonna gloat now, I hope," she murmured.

Taking one of the clean napkins, he said nothing as he gently wiped the wetness between her legs. Feeling at ease—maybe she was becoming accustomed to their times together—she found his attention to this small detail gentlemanly. She was glad not to have to endure the clamminess for the duration of the walk back to the Chateau.

He pulled the dress back over her legs. She eyed the wine in his glass. She'd need a few drinks to calm the energy she felt in her body right now. If she were a horse, she could've run a hundred laps.

Seeing the object of her gaze, he allowed her his glass, which she finished off. He rose to stretch his legs. She wanted to know if he needed anything. Certainly, the bulge in his pants indicated he required relief, but he made no move to seek it. Instead he went to pack up their basket. Had something happened to him since their encounter of a year ago? Was he no longer capable? Did he forget to bring protection? Did he not desire her enough? Unless he came with equal fervor, she felt unsatisfied.

Returning, he began to collect the items of their picnic.

"Back to the Chateau?" she asked.

"Yes."

Just as she was about to purse her lips at his taciturn manner, he looked at her, a gleam in his eyes. "After all, there is still the matter of your punishment."

CHAPTER 9

Fuck, *Halsten reiterated* to himself, his cock ready to bust the zipper off his pants. If not for marveling at the beauty of her climax, he would've thrown himself on her. Witnessing her orgasm was an acute turn-on. Nothing was more titillating or invigorating, except the act of fucking her. That he could produce such glorious screams and shudders from her was hella gratifying. The vision of her legs sprawled open, her back arched against him, her brows knitted in twisted pleasure on her uplifted face, was something he would replay in his mind over and over again. And, for a brief moment, he knew no other woman could elicit an equally intense response from him. He craved her more than anything.

After packing up their picnic, they walked in relative silence back to the Chateau, via a different route. He needed to concentrate on cooling his desires and kept his comments to the history of the land and extent of the estate.

The breeze had become stronger as they walked. Strands of hair flew around her cheeks, which, already flushed from their previous exchange, were now in ripe bloom. Her eyes sparkled, and her complexion glowed with bliss. He couldn't contain his ardor any longer, his guard crumbling like a weak dam against a strong flood. Seizing her, he crushed his mouth on hers. Her lips, soft and pliant, parted beneath his. He felt his blood pounding in all parts of his body—his head, his chest, and especially his groin. Pushing his tongue deep into her mouth, he tasted her. Wanting to consume her with all senses, he inhaled her scent, a nondescript but heady air that lengthened his cock. He pressed his erection against her, feeling as if he might explode if he didn't find a way to possess her from the inside.

Startled by the intensity of his assault, she offered no resistance. Instead, she pressed her own body against his. She moaned as he seared her neck with large, moist mouthfuls. Wanting to devour her, he licked and sucked his way back to her mouth. She grunted into his mouth at the force of his kiss. But this time it was not about her pleasure but his need to claim her body with his.

But through the storm he meant to unleash on her, he found enough restraint to allow her a breath. She gazed into his eyes, her pupils dilated. He confirmed that she didn't dislike the onslaught, though he had a momentary doubt as to whether he could stop no matter what her reaction—a troubling recognition that was lost in the surge of raw, animal desire for this woman.

His restraint, however, was tested by another source.

"Is that Halsten Rockwell?"

The voice was at some distance still, but he felt Deana stiffen in his arms immediately. He kept his gaze on her, but she'd turned to look toward the speaker. Steeling his nerves and suppressing the instinct to turn on the intruder with a vengeance, he managed to step away from Deana and compose himself. He heard two sets of footsteps approach but didn't turn around. He would only have glared at the interlopers.

"Halsten Rockwell?"

It was a woman's voice and one he recognized with great surprise.

eana saw the stunned look in the Rockwell's eyes before he turned around to greet the new company: a couple. The man, dressed as handsomely as Rockwell usually was, but with a less serious and more friendly demeanor, was accompanied by a beautiful young woman. Deana had thought her own dress looked nice, but the halter dress worn by the other woman with its A-line cut and unique floral print looked like something off a Paris runway. Maybe the wearer, with her delicate features and golden hair, was in fact a model.

"Bella," Rockwell greeted when the couple had stopped near them. His gaze shifted to the other man and there was no mistaking his stiffened tone. "Devon."

Devon, however, seemed oblivious or impervious to the cool welcome. His gaze fell on Deana. "And who is this?"

It was then that the woman seemed to notice the presence of another, and Deana detected a slight narrowing of the woman's eyes.

Rockwell looked at Deana for a moment before replying, "Deana."

Deana doubted that she'd cross paths with the couple outside Chateau Follet, as they were clearly more familiar with Rockwell's strata of society, but she was grateful that he didn't include her last name.

"Nice to meet you," Devon responded with a large grin. "Are you staying at Chateau Follet?"

"We are," Rockwell replied.

"So are we."

Rockwell's nostrils flared and he looked to Bella for confirmation. She regarded him carefully.

"I had no idea you knew Marguerite Follet," she remarked.

Observing the exchange between the two, Deana suspected Rockwell and Bella had been on familiar terms.

EM BROWN

"Likewise," Rockwell said.

They seemed to have forgotten the presence of the other two until Devon interjected, "Staying long?"

Rockwell's response was a curt "No."

Bella turned her attention once more to Deana. She seemed to take in every aspect of her appearance and determined that something had happened between her and Rockwell. Unperturbed, Deana returned the stare in full. This startled Bella and seemed to put Deana even lower in the woman's estimation.

"Have we met before?" Bella asked, narrowing her eyes a touch.

"That's doubtful," Deana replied, "unless you frequent poker rooms."

"I've never met a female poker player before," Devon said while Bella turned her gaze to Rockwell with a curious expression.

"Maybe we can get to know each other better at dinner?" Devon suggested, eying Deana with even more interest.

"Maybe," Rockwell said, his tone doubtful. "We haven't—"

"Sure," Deana said gaily, ignoring Rockwell's frown.

Devon gave a friendly mock-salute, and he and Bella turned around, continuing on one of the paths. Deana hurried toward the house. Knowing that Rockwell wasn't pleased, she wanted to put some distance between them. If she'd had more forethought, she might not have spoken as she had, but curiosity, and a little jealousy, won out. Jealousy wasn't a sentiment she was familiar with, but she hoped to overcome it for their remaining time at Chateau Follet.

Rockwell, folding his arms, caught up with her. "I didn't say that we would have dinner with them."

"You didn't forbid it. And I'd like to know why Bella doesn't seem too keen on me."

"You guys just met. All she did was ask you a question."

She looked at him with some sympathy. The most astute of

men couldn't discern the subtleties that women could. Strangely, the jealousy fueled her confidence.

"It was her tone."

"Bella is quick to judge," he admitted.

As she'd suspected, the two had been close. They walked in relative silence. Deana wondered if his thoughts were on Bella. She knew there was no real relationship between herself and Rockwell, as there probably had been between him and Bella, but she would've liked to have had him to herself for the rest of their time at Chateau Follet.

Rockwell allowed her some solitude before dinner. Then she got ready, slipping on an almost sheer gown with intricate embroidery that Bhadra must've left on her bed. It had a nude lining, so that not much beyond her cleavage showed, but in it, as it hugged her curves and gave the illusion of nakedness, she felt somewhat exposed.

Despite her curiosity, she would have preferred to have dinner without the extra company. She sighed at the new feelings Rockwell had engendered, for better and for worse. Anger and shyness, titillation and euphoria, brazenness and jealousy. What a mix of emotions for one day! And throughout it all, a thrill unique to anything she'd felt before.

Bhadra returned to make sure she was ready. Deana took the opportunity to satisfy her curiosity, and maybe quench her own nerves by focusing on someone else. "Do you miss India at all?"

After a pause, Bhadra replied, "I like it here."

Though she'd spoken in a noncommittal way, Deana respected her reserved nature and didn't press for more details.

"Would you like help with your hair?" Bhadra asked.

Deana nodded. It had gotten wind-blown earlier. Bhadra worked her magic, curling and smoothing, putting it up in a loose bun.

"I'm just grateful to be in a country where I can choose my future," she said after some silence.

The sentiment tugged at Deana's heart.

"Do you have any family back in India?"

Bhadra nodded. "My grandfather, an aunt and uncle."

Deana had a dozen questions at the tip of her tongue, but as this was the most the other woman had spoken in one spell, she let Bhadra dictate the pace.

"Mr. Rockwell offered to bring my family here, but my grandfather is too old to make the journey, and my aunt and uncle preferred to say in India. They are very old-fashioned. Even more than my parents."

"That was kind of Rockwell to offer to do that."

"He's been more than generous."

Bhadra spoke with a wistfulness that made Deana suspect that the woman had some tender feelings toward Rockwell. She considered her own experiences with the man and his gift to her of the ivory elephant.

"He had no reason to help a stranger, which I was to him at the time," Bhadra added.

Rockwell appeared before Deana could ask anything else, dressed casually in a button up shirt, blazer, and khakis. Deana felt a twinge of vanity knowing that she'd be escorted to dinner by such a good-looking man. From his appreciative appraisal of her, she could be satisfied that she wasn't so bad herself. He presented his arm. She slid her own between its crook, her heart beating a little more rapidly. Maybe it was the dress, or his fine manners, or the triumph that came from having pleased his eye when he probably crossed paths with women who had more elegance, that made her feel rather like a princess.

The dining room proved more intimate than Deana predicted from such a stately structure, but she found the room appealing. The table was adorned simply with two vases of roses spaced perfectly so as not to obstruct view and conversation across the table and china that gleamed with luxury but avoided the ostentatious. The proprietress, wearing a feathered tocque and large gold hoop earrings, presided at the head of the table. To her left sat a pretty young woman who seemed to have eyes only for Marguerite. To her right sat a buff man wearing a tight shirt. Beside him was a brunette who couldn't stop giggling.

Though she didn't think she'd find anyone she knew, Deana was relieved to find her hope confirmed. After seeing her to her chair, Rockwell took his seat opposite her. Devon and Bella were similarly situated across the table from one another with the former beside Deana and the latter beside Rockwell. Deana couldn't help wonder if that had been by design. A server came to pour her a glass of wine. She glanced at Rockwell, who nodded his head ever so slightly.

Sitting across the table, Bella appeared nothing short of radiant in a gown of embroidered silk, breasts pushed high over the sweetheart neckline. She leaned in close to Rockwell and spoke in low tones. Unable to hear, Deana could only observe Rockwell respond with equal intimacy. Bella smiled. Deana took a long sip of her wine.

"So, Deana," Bella said, "I was thinking about your earlier remark. It sounds like you do a lot of gambling?"

Bella arched a shapely eyebrow. Deana smiled politely. "It's a hobby."

"You must be quite accomplished," Devon noted.

"Lady Luck has been nice to me more often than not."

She felt but avoided the gaze of Rockwell.

"A hobby? Not like an addiction," Bella commented, making it sound like she thought it anything but interesting, before turning to Rockwell. "I didn't know you hung out at gambling places."

"You ever play poker?" Devon asked Bella.

Ignoring him, Bella purred, "Tell us more about yourself, Deana. You sound … interesting."

"Actually, I'm pretty *uninteresting*."

"That would be insulting Rockwell's taste. And he is a man of taste. Trust me, I know."

Devon poked Bella in the ribs. "Does that mean you have taste, too, since you guys used to date?"

Bella frowned for a second but regained her composure. "Don't worry, Deana, that was a while ago. Rockwell obviously has entirely different interests now."

At that moment, a toast to Marguerite was proposed.

"To our lovely mistress of Chateau Follet. Our gratitude for your hospitality," said an older guy.

They all raised a glass to Marguerite. Deana took a hearty gulp. At another time, she would've savored the quality burgundy, but she barely tasted it. She was, at least, relieved from the attentions of Bella during the first and second courses. Rockwell looked at her often, but she couldn't tell his thoughts.

The wine flowed freely throughout dinner, and Deana noticed Bella laughing often and loudly, leaning in many times toward Rockwell, close enough to touch him. Deana reminded herself she had no cause to be jealous. She had no claims on him, not even for the time that they were at the Chateau. But rather than witness Bella fawning over Rockwell, Deana turned to Devon.

"Are you new to Chateau Follet?" Deana asked Devon.

"*Au contraire*. I'm a frequent guest," Devon responded proudly. "So tell me about yourself. You play anything besides poker?"

"Poker is my main interest."

"Maybe you could teach me a thing or two about the game."

Glancing across the table, she saw Rockwell eyeing her with a frown. She dismissed his look and turned her attentions back to Devon. "There are no quick tricks. It all depends on the cards you hold and what your opponents show."

"This is why I have no talent with cards. Too many variables! Anyway, I prefer more … *active* pursuits."

"Sports?" she offered, though she knew full well what he meant by the salacious gleam in his eyes.

"Of a kind."

He grinned at her and leaned toward her. She could smell the alcohol on his breath. A server came by to fill her glass. She saw Rockwell shake his head. Bella chose that moment to put her hand on his shoulder and whisper into his ear. Deana decided to ignore him and allowed her glass to be filled.

"Enjoying your stay here so far?" Devon asked her.

She wondered if she should encourage the drunken attentions of the man, but he had a friendly manner and the redhead sitting on the other side of her showed no interest in conversation as the woman had her head in the lap of her companion.

"The place is beautiful, and this dinner is amazing," she replied to Devon.

"And the people? Has our friend Rockwell been a skilled host?"

Deana took a sip of wine to avoid answering. She was also saved by the dessert service.

Distracted, Devon forgot his question and instead asked, "Are you staying in the West or the East Wing, Miss Sherwood?"

"West."

Her answer attracted the attention of Bella. She raised a brow at Rockwell. "Only the West Wing? Afraid to try the East Wing?"

"Are you in the East Wing?" he returned with surprise.

"Of course," Devon answered. "I never bother with the West Wing anymore."

Rockwell looked at Bella with greater surprise. She blushed.

Bella turned to Deana, "Maybe you'd like to join us?"

"We aren't staying long," Rockwell said with a tightness that confirmed he was not too keen on Devon.

Realizing that her companion had been conversing too much with Deana, Bella split her attentions between the two men for the rest of dinner. Deana was content to ignore the looks of admonition from Rockwell despite the warning from her wiser self that she was being foolish. She knew he wasn't pleased and suspected it had to do with the nature of the relationship between Bella and Devon. Well, she didn't intend to be the recipient of his frustrations over Bella.

When dinner had concluded and the guests had risen to their feet, Devon turned to Deana. "If I can convince Marguerite to bring out her card tables, would you want to play?"

Bella wavered and had to grasp Rockwell's arm to steady herself.

Deana smiled at Devon. "Why not?"

Rockwell's jaw hardened. "Deana and I had other plans."

Bella frowned. "The night is young yet."

Marguerite intervened. "Bella, I heard your father was a patron of the arts. Would you want to view my private collection of paintings?"

Even in her inebriated state, Bella was too polite to refuse her hostess.

Deana wondered if she, too, should attempt to persuade Rockwell to join the rest of the party, but her thoughts were slowed by the wine. She felt Devon at her elbow.

"My invitation is open," he purred. "If you want more excitement, the East Wing's got it in spades. Rockwell is no stranger there, but his presence isn't exactly required."

They both looked up to see Rockwell staring down at them. Devon cleared his throat and sauntered to where Bella stood. Rockwell extended his arm, which Deana took reluctantly.

She swore to herself. It was obvious Rockwell wasn't happy.

CHAPTER 10

D eana had defied him twice. Blatantly.

As they walked back to her room, Halsten attempted to calm the boiling of his blood. She wasn't wholly responsible for his discontent, he admitted, but she'd seen his disapproval and willfully ignored him, drinking freely and encouraging the attentions of that slimeball, Devon. Devon had a thing for virgins and younger looking women. The last time he and Devon happened to be staying at Chateau Follet at the same time, Devon had a sub who might even have been jailbait. One of Marguerite's staff had complained that twice she had a bewildered sub on her hands because Devon forget to provide any aftercare. How had Bella and Devon gotten together?

He'd tried to ascertain the answer to that question during dinner, but Bella had been hell-bent on flirting. That she could so easily disengage her attentions from Devon to himself eased his concerns a little, but her unexpected appearance at the Chateau had him taken aback. He recalled when they had dated briefly and couldn't identify anything that would lead him to believe her a candidate for the Chateau Follet.

The daughter of a wealthy businessman who had been a close

friend of Halsten's father and a mentor to him, Bella Collingsworth could attract just about any man. She had enticed him initially but then cooled toward him. In retrospect, she might simply have been playing hard to get, encouraging and then rebuffing him to increase his desire for her. Halsten had little patience for games like that.

In contrast, Deana's guileless manner appealed to him. However, she wouldn't be the first to appear artless. Or the first to want him for what he could give her. Her situation made him have doubts about whether she partly liked him for his money, which wasn't a concern with someone like Bella. But try as he might, he simply couldn't get Deana out of his mind.

Remembering the easy manner in which she spoke with Devon, he said, "I don't want you talking to Devon."

She stopped. He knew that she wouldn't be receptive to his demand, but he couldn't resist the effects of jealousy.

"It's in your best interest," he added. "He's no good for anyone."

"Because he might scandalize me?" she replied. "He wouldn't be the only one."

He felt the heat rise above his neck.

"Don't worry about me," she said. "I've come across guys worse than Devon. Your efforts might be better spent protecting Bella. She seems to need your attention."

He'd wanted to issue just such a caution to Bella, and he fully intended to speak with her at a more sober moment. He'd made a promise to her late father to look out for her. He wondered when to seek her out and remembered that Devon had referenced the East Wing. *Shit. Did Bella know what lay in store in the East Wing?*

Gauging his thoughts, Deana said, "She's really pretty."

"She has more looks than sense," he thought aloud, but feeling himself closer to the true subject of discussion, turned the focus back on Deana. "You shouldn't have encouraged Devon's attentions."

"It would've been rude not to speak to him, and as you and Bella were engaged, I had few options."

The truth of her statement didn't satisfy him. "You know the rules."

"You'd rather I sit and twiddle my fingers?"

"Yes. You're not supposed to flirt with anyone without my permission."

"What happens in the East Wing, exactly?"

He reached for her to lead her back to her room. "Nothing you need to bother with."

She eluded his grasp. "I'm curious to see it."

He felt a tug at his groin. "You are far from ready to be in the East Wing."

"Bella is a new guest."

"If Devon had a considerate bone in his body, they wouldn't be in the East Wing."

He took her by the elbow and guided her back to her room, more harshly than he'd intended. The thought of Bella in the East Wing made him angry. Spoiled by her father growing up, Bella wasn't adept at making the best choices.

"I'll be back in half an hour," he told her once they'd reached her bedroom. "Do you want me to send Bhadra up to keep you company?"

"That won't be necessary."

Her curious gaze at him suggested she wanted to understand his intentions, but he was too agitated to delay the night with explanations.

"Half an hour," he repeated.

"Is that a promise or a warning?"

"Both," he growled.

Yanking her to him, he smothered her mouth for emphasis. He worked her mouth in selfish consumption, his ardor fueled by irritation. His tongue delved deep and he paid no attention to the fine lines of her lips. When he was done, the kiss had blurred and dampened her lipstick.

"Half an hour then," she murmured between uneven breaths.

She stepped inside and closed the door slowly between them. He stood on the threshold, tempted to throw open the door and ravish her mouth once more. But he couldn't leave Bella to her own devices. She'd seemed pretty drunk. With quick strides, he caught up with the group as they made their way through the halls of the East Wing, admiring the many erotic paintings that hung there.

"This painter adored the fleshy figures of Reuben," Marguerite explained as they stood before a full-length painting of a woman standing naked beneath a waterfall, the water splashing over her heavy breasts.

He came up to Bella. "We need to talk."

Devon turned around with the intention of objecting, but Halsten silenced him with an icy stare. Devon moved on with the group as they strolled to the next painting of two men bathing.

"Where's your date?" Bella asked with an arched brow.

Ignoring her question, he said in a low and firm voice, "This is no place for you, Bella."

She fluttered her skirt, the upward quirk of her mouth indicated she was enjoying his attention. "You don't know me well enough to make such a statement."

He had to acknowledge the truth of what she said. He would never have supposed her to be one open to the activities at Chateau Follet. Had he known, he might have continued his pursuit of her.

"You don't know what goes on here," he countered. "The East Wing here is no place for a novice."

She tried to look confident, but her flash of fear told him the truth. "You coming to rescue me then?"

"You need to rethink this. Devon isn't as nice as you might think."

She tapped her finger against his upper arm and gave him a teasing look that would've melted many a man. "Not like you to be jealous, Halsten. You gave me up easily enough before."

He took in a deep breath. "Please, Bella. I'm doing this for you."

She smiled. "For little old *moi?*"

"How do you know Devon anyway?"

"You remember my friend Robyn Goodall? She introduced me to Devon."

He didn't remember this woman, but he wouldn't trust the keenness of anyone who recommended Devon.

"You should go home, Bella."

She rolled her eyes. Home for her was in Atherton, several hours away. "Why?"

He couldn't tell if her resistance stemmed from her headstrong ways or from pure foolishness. If he could, he'd take her home himself.

"I know that serious look," she laughed. "But I like that you're trying to be my knight in shining armor."

A muscle along his jaw tightened. "Bella—"

"What are you two whispering about?" Devon interrupted as he came up to them, having torn himself away from the group. "She's my date, in case you've forgotten, Rockwell. What happened to yours?"

Recalling that he'd assured Deana that he'd return within half an hour, he suppressed the desire to deck the man just for the hell of it. He turned to Bella.

"I'm here if you need me."

As he made his way back to the West Wing, Halsten shook his head. How the hell was he going to convince Bella of the sense of what he said? A part of him wanted to stay with her and keep his eye on Devon, but then he'd be a poor host to Deana.

And he had unfinished business with her.

Frustration with Bella and anger with Devon had already

riled him, and as he neared Deana's bedroom, he was fit to burst. He knocked on the door and didn't wait for a reply. He found her sitting on the sofa, but she rose to her feet on his entrance. Closing the door behind him, he lost no time. He strode to her.

Surprised by the swiftness of his actions, Deana made no movement and only stared. His palm itched to spank that precious ass of hers, but what he intended required patience.

He reached for her, molding her body to his. His lips grazed her neck. He slid his tongue lightly along the side of it.

"You've been extremely disobedient, my pet."

She gasped when he took a mouthful of her neck. "If you want a meek and obedient woman, I'm surprised that you want me."

At times he wondered as well. He'd never doubted her independence and willfulness, which bordered on brash even, but these qualities only enhanced his interest in her.

"You're not in Gabby's club," he said as he moved his lips over hers, "but on my grounds. So you'll adhere to my rules."

"I feel sorry for the woman who ends up marrying you someday," she murmured against his mouth.

For some reason her statement irritated him. He grasped her buttock and squeezed it hard. Her eyes flew open. Heat swirled around his groin. He spun her around and began unzipping her gown.

"If you're interested in the East Wing, you have to prove yourself first," he informed her as he yanked the garment down her arms.

The dress was easily dispensed with. Standing in only her bra, thong, and thigh-high stockings, she shivered, though Bhadra, as he'd instructed before leaving for dinner, had a strong fire burning in the fireplace. He ran a knuckle between her shoulder blades and admired the contours of her upper back.

"How?" she inquired as he undid her bra.

"You'll see soon enough."

He undid her bra. Reaching around with both hands, he

palmed each breast. The amount of wine she'd consumed was enough to lower her inhibitions. She leaned back against him and arched herself further into his hands. He kneaded each mound and felt her nipples harden. He pulled and pinched the rosy nubs, making her groan, as his own head swam with the possibilities. She had a strong, beautiful body. If she proved tolerant, there was much he could do to her, with her.

He slid the thong down her legs. Slipping his hand between her thighs, he found her already wet with desire. He stroked her there until she whimpered and ground herself against him. Her ass pressed against his cock, which stretched toward her. How easy it would be to unbutton his pants and ram his cock into her ass. To cool the temptation, he stepped away from her and went to one of the armoires to retrieve coils of rope and a cat-o-nine tails. Her lips parted slightly but she was no stranger to the items. She'd enjoyed them greatly in the past.

"Take off the stockings," he instructed as he rolled up his sleeves.

With lust shining in her eyes, she did as he said and slid the nylon down her legs. She stood before him completely naked, a little more at ease than before. Once more he swept his gaze appreciatively over her body. His cock pulsed, wanting action. He sauntered over to her and looked into her eyes, confirming that she wanted him as much as he wanted her. He brushed his fingers gently along her collarbone and kissed her shoulder.

Then his demeanor changed. Thrusting his hand into her hair, he yanked on the loose coils to force her chin up, then smothered her mouth with his. She yelped but yielded to the assault on her mouth. He dug deep into the warm, wet crevice with his tongue. Her breathing became heavy against his upper lip and he smelled the wine from dinner. He would taste of her in as many ways possible before they left, he promised himself. Fire consumed his veins and he disengaged himself abruptly for as much his sake as hers.

"Lie down on the bed."

Still breathless from the kiss, she took a moment but complied, with a touch of awkwardness. He stretched her arms overhead and bound her wrists to the bedposts with the rope, then did the same with her ankles till her body formed an 'X' with each limb tethered to a bedpost. Stepping back, he admired his handiwork. *Damn.* He could see the glisten of wetness between her legs.

She pulled at her bonds, but the ropes had little give. He could see that she felt ill at ease being spread and exposed that way.

"Remember the safeword?" he asked as he retrieved the tails.

"Rati," she said, the name of the goddess coming from deep in her throat.

Even her speech affected him, and he couldn't give blame to the wine as he'd consumed only two glasses in the course of the evening. He steeled his nerves. What he was about to do to her required a steady hand.

"Your punishment begins."

He passed a hand from her toes and up her leg, past her hip and ribcage, and up to the bottom of a breast. He cupped it tenderly. It had a lovely shape to it and large areolas. He leaned down and put his mouth on the puckered nipple. A tiny purr escaped her. He swirled his tongue over it and gently sucked. Her toes curled in response. He flicked his tongue at the nipple, licked it and pulled it until she twisted in her bonds. He reached a hand to her groin, grazing the hair between her legs and sliding a finger against her clit. She emitted a shaky groan. While attending to the nipple, he fingered that other nub and occasionally slipped his finger into her hot, soaking pussy. Her body arched off the bed.

Satisfied that he had her sufficiently aroused, he stepped back and unfurled the tails. He whipped them against the side of her breast, careful to avoid the nipple. She cried out, mostly in surprise. He lashed again at the breast. The mound of flesh quivered at the impact. She sucked at the air. This time he knew it stung a little. He slapped the tails against her inner thigh. Her leg wanted to recoil but was held in place by the bindings. He slapped her there again, and she gasped at how close he had come to striking her cunt.

"Please," she murmured.

"Use your safeword if you have to, but you'll have to endure a lot more if you want to enter the East Wing."

At that, she closed her mouth and awaited his next move. He applied the tails to her other breast until the skin blushed. She cried out each time but didn't call out the name of Rati. The moisture at her sex increased.

He applied the flogger lightly to her ribs then let the tails fall once on her pussy. She would've leapt off the bed if she hadn't been held down by the bindings. He rubbed her between her legs.

"Think you've learned your lesson?"

"Hmph?" she responded through a haze of arousal and vexation.

"What have we learned?"

"To obey."

"To obey what?"

"Your orders."

"Without delay."

"Yes, sir."

He wanted to tell her that she'd only take pleasure from him, that she belonged to him. She was his alone to command and gratify and protect. But these were dangerous feelings to have. Voicing them might make them less fleeting.

"And if you please me, I might reward you."

"Yes, sir."

He stroked her wet folds with his thumb. Her body, already near the height, didn't require long to go over the precipice. As she came, she bucked off the bed and writhed violently against the ropes. He didn't wait for her to completely descend from her climax and dove once more between her legs.

Confused, she seemed to not know whether she wanted the continued attention. He suspected her pussy was by now exceedingly sensitive. It pulsed hot and wet beneath his mouth. She attempted to move away from him, but he grasped her hips and held her in place. He didn't relent and soon had her riding a second wave of ecstasy. Screaming, she succumbed to the stimulation with such forceful spasms that she struck him in the chin. He rubbed her gently until the last of her shivers subsided and she let out a deep sigh. For a while he gazed at her as she recovered herself, drinking in the sight of her stretched across the bed, her breasts still bearing the markings of the flogger, her body flush from the experience.

Damn, he wanted to fuck her.

CHAPTER 11

A fter untying her and rubbing a pomade on the places where the nine-tail had landed, he pulled the covers over Deana as sleep overtook her. He smoothed his clothes and stepped softly to the door. He turned at the threshold to look at her in peaceful slumber, her hair spread over the pillows, one bare arm curled above her head. If he didn't leave soon, he might be tempted to wake her to relieve the bulge at his crotch. Forcing himself through the door, he tried not to recall how she'd looked stretched to the bedposts in glorious nakedness, her sweet sex open to him like a blossom to the sun.

When he'd first invited her to Chateau Follet, he had mostly selfish reasons. He wanted another taste of her body. He wanted to satisfy his own lust. But ever since her acceptance, her pleasure had become the dominant priority. He took much enjoyment from seeing her come and surprised himself that he hadn't yet fucked her for his own sake.

And now another woman took him from attending to his own needs.

He made his way back to the East Wing and headed straight for the ballroom in search of Bella. The ballroom was the focus of activity for the East Wing. Hearty flames crackled from all four fireplaces and provided much of the low light desired by the hostess. The chandeliers above were kept dim, allowing for pockets of darkness throughout the room. Lush sofas lined the walls beneath erotic paintings and golden candelabras. The center of the room, however, looked more like a medieval dungeon with body racks, wooden pommels, an iron cage, and other furnishings of torture.

Bella sat on one of the sofas beside Devon. She'd had more wine in the meantime as evidenced by her shining eyes, flush cheeks, and constant giggling. Her partner, too, was happily inebriated and attempting to devour her neck. He had her legs across his thighs.

"Rockwell!" Bella exclaimed as she tried to right herself without spilling the wine from the glass she held.

Devon sat up and tried to focus his gaze on Halsten in the darkness. "Rockwell? Where's Deana?"

"Resting," Halsten replied, grimly staring at Devon. "One shouldn't extend the abilities of a novice at Chateau Follet."

"Is Miss Sherwood the inexperienced one or *you?*" Bella teased.

"Have a drink with us," Devon invited. "Maybe a good shot of whiskey will give you the balls you need."

Biting his tongue, Halsten pulled up a chair as Devon motioned to one of the servers. A young naked woman approached them with shots of vodka and whiskey on her tray. Devon ogled the woman as she handed him a shot of whiskey.

"Hot, isn't she?" Devon purred into Bella's ear.

Bella giggled. "She must get cold in the winter."

"Their nipples are constantly erect."

He pretended to pinch one of hers. Bella swatted at his hand and laughed. She seemed to notice the serious look Halsten gave her and stopped.

Devon followed her gaze. "Why so serious? Bring that date of yours here. You'll be a happier man."

Halsten forced his mouth from a frown even as he retorted silently that he wouldn't bring Deana within an arm's length of Devon.

"That won't be necessary," he said. "I'm fine watching."

"I've no problem with that." He raised a glass at Halsten.

Bella struck Devon playfully across the chest. "You're joking!"

"Devon didn't mention that he's a fan of exhibitionism?" Halsten asked her.

Her eyebrows rose at Devon.

"I promise, it's very exciting," Devon told her.

Hers was a nervous smile.

"To Chateau Follet," Halsten said, raising his glass.

"To Chateau Follet," Devon echoed, throwing down his whiskey in one gulp.

Halsten, who'd taken several glasses from the server, offered Devon another.

A bell chimed, drawing their attention to a clearing in the center of the ballroom. A woman lay naked on a long table. Her dominant, wearing only a pair of pants, announced, "I'm pleased to share my submissive with the honored guests of Chateau Follet."

"No!" Bella cried out in surprise, covering her collagen injected lips with her slender hand.

"Hell, yes," Devon growled beneath his breath as he downed another shot.

The Dominant spread the woman's legs open as curious and willing guests approached the couple. A woman with silver in her hair knelt at the submissive's cunt.

"I can't look!" Bella giggled and hid her face in Devon's chest.

The older woman licked the submissive. Having stolen a peek, Bella shrieked.

"I'm not a fan of the smell of cunt, but there's nothing like seeing a woman eat another woman's pussy," Devon commented.

Bella seemed to vacillate between embarrassment and curiosity, carelessly sipping her wine as she gazed on the center of the ballroom. Her eyes seemed oddly glassy.

She shook her head. "I could never—"

For a moment, Halsten wondered if Deana would submit to the touch of another woman. The image of her spread on the table before another woman made the blood at his groin churn.

The submissive began moaning and writhing on the table.

"A sight, isn't it?" Halsten directed at Devon.

Devon pulled at his collar. "Yes."

"How can she ... enjoy that?" Bella asked.

"This is tame compared to what Devon has seen and done," Halsten said. "Haven't you had as many as three women at once, Devon?"

The effects of the liquor on him, Devon hesitated, but conscious of Bella's gaze on him, he waved a dismissive hand. "That's the past. Bella is worth at least three women."

Bella smiled while Halsten frowned.

"Your date surprises me, Halsten," she said. "Deana's not exactly in your league. I would've thought you could do better."

Anger flashed in Halsten, but Deana could defend herself. It wasn't his place to protect her in this. "There's more to her than meets the eye."

"Even Vivian Chen would have been better."

Her remark surprised him since she and Vivian used to be good friends. He hadn't known Bella to be so petty before. Was she jealous? Either way, Bella obviously didn't see Deana's true beauty, as he did. "She's not as lucky as you, Bella," he said and held up his glass to her.

She beamed.

"To beautiful women," Devon toasted.

They finished off their drinks. Halsten motioned to the server for more.

They watched as others took their turn with the submissive. One man fondled her breasts while another woman locked lips with her. While pretending to be engaged in the exhibition, Halsten kept a steady eye on Devon and Bella. He ensured Devon had plenty to drink. The alcohol made Devon more libidinous but also impaired his motions. Since she didn't weigh that much, Bella couldn't withstand the effects of drinking for long and began to fall into a stupor.

"I need the bathroom," Bella grumbled.

"I'll take you," said Halsten, already upon his feet.

Devon waved his hand, his vacant-eyed gaze fixed across the room on two women engaged in a strenuous kiss.

Bella stared at Halsten's outstretched hand. When she made no further movement, he hoisted her to her feet by her waist. As he assisted her from the room, he motioned to one of the staff.

"Have her attendant sent to her room," he instructed.

Bella's arm slipped from around his shoulder and she sank to the floor.

"This floor is not working," she murmured.

After she struggled to stand, he decided it was simpler to carry her.

"Ohhh, I don't feel right ..." she grimaced and put a hand to her mouth.

Once inside the ensuite bathroom, he set her down in front of the toilet. She retched and spilled the contents of her stomach. Mortified, she covered her mouth once more.

"Get it all out," he instructed her.

Again, she heaved. She gagged but only bile remained. He handed her his handkerchief. With a groan, she sat back.

Spotting the attendant, he instructed, "She is *not* to leave her room tonight." He doubted Devon would care about Bella's consent at this point. If he ever cared.

EM BROWN

The woman nodded. With a last glance at the groaning Bella, he shook his head and left the room.

Shit. Bella was worse than Lucille. God help Lucille if he ever discovered that his sister ever behaved as recklessly; he'd lock her in her room till she was thirty.

Bella, however, wasn't his sister. How far did his promise to the late Collingsworth really extend? Being responsible for Bella had cut into his time with Deana. If it weren't for Bella, he would've been in bed with Deana. He imagined his body entwined with hers. He wondered if she was awake.

He decided to see for himself if she was. Back at the threshold to her room, he quietly opened the door. The last flickers of the flames in the fireplace provided a sufficient glow for him to see. Deana lay serenely asleep in her bed under the plush covers. He shouldn't disturb her peaceful rest, but his cock had reared its head at the sight of her. Recalling how she'd felt in his arms, how soft her skin had felt beneath his hands, he couldn't move himself to leave.

As if sensing his presence, she stirred. Her eyes opened halfway. A smile flitted across her lips. She stretched and opened her eyes more.

"Back for more?" she asked.

There was no leaving now. He'd denied his need long enough. He began to tug off his shirt. She sat up against the pillows and watched as he placed the linen at the foot of the bed. He unbuttoned and shed his pants next. He walked over to the side of the bed and threw the covers off of her. Instinctively, she covered herself with her arms and hands. He could see a few bites of the nine-tail on her breasts.

He put one knee on the bed and moved her arm off her chest. "God, you're beautiful."

Grasping her chin, he pulled her to him and pressed his mouth to hers. He inhaled the smell of her as he worked his lips and tongue over her, each taste increasing his appetite and enflaming his body. He had to have her. And possess her he would.

Circling an arm around her waist, he crushed her body to his. His erection pressed hard against her. He was tempted to take her without foreplay. Feeling between her legs, he found a wetness there that couldn't have been simply from their prior encounter. Her desire was more than intoxicating. With a groan, he delved his tongue into her mouth. He fondled her clit till she panted against his mouth, struggling slightly to keep up with the onslaught.

His cock stretched, more than anxious to merge with her hot, wet pussy. He slipped on a condom. When one of her hands wrapped around his neck and buried itself in his hair, he moved closer to her. Lips still locked, he leaned her back into the bed and lay on top of her. He could feel her breasts pushing into his chest and her glorious wetness seeping onto his thigh. He kissed her harder. As always, she tasted divine.

He took her nipples next. His ardor wouldn't allow him more delicacy and he sucked them forcefully, making her gasp and writhe under him. He was relieving his impatience and the stress of the evening through her, but if she weren't so damned alluring, he might've found it easier to be less demanding. Instead he ground his cock into her as if he'd been waiting years for her. And, in a way, he had been.

"Take me."

At first, he barely heard her, but when he looked into her eyes, she repeated her words.

"Take me."

Her gaze seemed to challenge him. He didn't need more of an invitation. His cock sprang at the ready. He rubbed its head against her folds, so deliciously wet. Her eyelashes fluttered, and a purr escaped her lips. He pushed against her opening, and she tilted her hips for him. With as much patience as he could muster, he pushed the head of his shaft into her. She gasped at the intrusion, her muscles pulsing about him. He sank himself further into her. She moaned.

"Damn," he breathed when he'd buried himself to the hilt.

The heat. The moisture. It had been too long. How had he managed to stay away from this for a year? He should've been inside of her sooner.

She wrapped her arms around his neck. He began to slide in and out of her, slowly and carefully. He needed to steel himself against coming too early. She met his every thrust, and they began to build a steady rhythm. Once he felt himself in control, he palmed a breast and brushed his thumb over her nipple. He propped himself up to view her face, her eyelids lowered, and her cheeks flushed.

He speared into her with increasing force while ensuring his angle produced the maximum response from her. Their rhythm quickened, and she grasped his biceps to keep herself in place. Her moans turned into cries as her wave began to build. He pushed against her, wanting to become one with her body. There was nothing finer than being buried inside of her, enveloped in her desire. He relished the feel of her naked body. He squeezed the breast he held as the fire in his scrotum threatened to boil over.

With a wail, she bucked and shuddered violently beneath him. Her fingers dug into him, but he felt only the pressure of desire from his groin. With a low grunt, he pushed himself into her as deep as he could go. His muscles tightened, then released with a series of convulsions as he spilled himself into her. He thrust at her a few more times until the last of the tremors had subsided. Relief washed through him from head to toe.

Damn. It felt as magnificent as the first time.

He kissed her below her ear before pulling out of her. Rolling onto his side, he collected her in his arms. She nestled against his chest with a satisfied sigh. He closed his eyes. For the moment, he forgot all else except for how it felt to hold her in his arms.

Deana woke earlier than usual but felt she'd slept deeply. She opened her eyes and found herself alone. She'd been somewhat aware of his leaving her bed in the middle of the night but had been too tired to pay much attention. As she stretched, memories of last night flooded her immediately. Rockwell had untied her bindings with a tenderness that contrasted with the sharpness of his discipline. From her vanity, he'd retrieved and applied a pomade to the marks on her sensitive breasts. She cupped an orb and felt a tug between her legs. She trailed a hand there, remembering how delightful his attentions had been. She rolled her clit between her fingers, amazed at how quickly her arousal had flamed. Would she always find herself in such a heightened state while at the Chateau or in the company of Rockwell?

And then he'd returned and taken her at last. She felt satisfied at the soreness between her legs. She'd begun to wonder why he hadn't entered her before. When he finally did, it had felt *amazing*. With her previous lovers, she hadn't always come, occasionally faking an orgasm. There was no faking with Rockwell, no need to at all.

With thoughts of him, she fondled herself until she came. Despite the release, she felt hungry for more. Rather, she felt hungry for *him*. Throwing back the covers, she decided to start the morning and attempt normalcy in spite of the setting. She'd survived one day and needed to last two more. She rang for Bhadra and went to the bathroom to refresh herself.

Bhadra appeared with a breakfast tray in hand.

"Is Rockwell awake?" Deana asked as she selected a simple cotton dress for the morning.

"He's on the veranda overlooking the garden. He asked me to let him know when you are up."

"He isn't making a habit of entering unannounced?" Deana

couldn't help herself and saw Bhadra suppress a grin. "Rich men think they can do anything they want."

"But he's a good man."

Having spoken, perhaps more than intended, Bhadra quickly busied herself by asking after her needs. Deana understood Bhadra's quick defense of Rockwell and didn't press her.

After dressing and finishing her breakfast, Deana went downstairs in search of Rockwell. As Bhadra had indicated, he was on the veranda. He sat at a table with his cell in hand, his brow furrowed in thought. Treading lightly, she had the opportunity to admire him without his notice. He'd allowed his hair to grow since their appointment of a year ago. Today it had a wind-swept appearance and she was tempted to run her fingers through it.

He looked up and the lines around his face eased. He set his phone down. "Good morning."

She smiled. "Good morning. Don't let me interrupt."

"Stay." He gestured to the teapot and cups on the table. "Coffee or tea?"

She joined him at the table and saw that he had been in the middle of a long text.

As if seeing the subject of her gaze, he said, "My younger sister. She's sixteen, and I'm her guardian."

Recalling his look of concern earlier, she said, "Is everything okay?"

"I guess," he replied unconvincingly.

"You don't sound very confident about that."

"She's … stubborn."

He shook his head but there was affection in his tone.

"Better stubborn than meek," Deana said.

"That remains to be seen."

"You'd rather she relent to others without fighting for herself?"

"Where I'm concerned, yes. I have her best interests at heart. I've told her that a dozen times, but she still doesn't get it."

He got up and walked to the railing.

"I know something about stubborn young women. May I?"

He hesitated at first but then nodded. She picked up his phone and read through the text he had been composing.

"Your tone feels … didactic," she commented. She never thought she would use that word.

He seemed taken aback, then waved a dismissive hand. "Sure. That's just because I'm older and more experienced."

"I don't know your sister but telling someone you know better usually doesn't work. Especially with teenagers."

"She wants to go to Mexico with some guy she met last summer. They barely know each other."

Deana could not help but find his irritation and confusion rather charming. "Does she love you?"

Her question baffled him, but he answered, "Yes."

"And respect you?"

"To an extent."

"Respect and obedience aren't the same."

"If she had complete respect for me, she wouldn't challenge me on this."

"Maybe if she feared you, yes. That she does feel comfortable speaking her mind to you is actually a good thing."

"She isn't being rational. I've been in the world a lot longer than she has. And she went to an all-girls boarding school. She doesn't know all that much about teenage boys. Whereas I …"

"But you can't lock your sister in a bubble. Try to see it from her side."

"I'm not letting her go to Mexico so she can wind up on someone's teens-gone-wild video."

She hadn't seen him this upset before. The prudent course would be to change the subject, but she wasn't ready to retreat.

"I'm not suggesting you should let her go to Mexico, but you might want to try and find some common ground. If you just say she can't go and that's that, she might start to resent you."

He had his arms crossed and looked at her solemnly. She had intended to be helpful, but maybe she'd overstepped her bounds. She decided to pour herself a cup of tea. The beverage was no longer hot, but she drank it anyway.

"Do you speak from experience?" he asked.

"What young person hasn't rebelled against their parent or guardian at some time? Don't be so afraid to trust her a little."

His features softened, and his posture relaxed. He sat back down at the table but continued to appraise her. "Okay. You're quite insightful."

His compliment took her by surprise. Coming from a man as confident and worldly as he, it was no small statement.

"If that's so, it's only because I've been through a lot of trial and error."

When she looked up from her cup, she found him staring at her with an expression she couldn't place. As with that night in the rain beneath the umbrella, the world seemed to have shrunk to the space between them. Resisting the moment and surge of emotion in her, she turned her attention to the wonderful view of the garden, lush with spring blooms and ripe lemon trees.

He followed her gaze. "Would you like to see the garden?"

She nodded. "Since it looks like it'll be another nice day, maybe we could walk again later?"

He paused before saying, "Let's see the garden first."

Rising to his feet, he took his phone and deleted the text he had been composing. They strolled the garden in comfortable silence. Between the birds chirping overhead and the trellises covered in wisteria, Deana felt as if she were in another world. And the quiet between her and Rockwell was kind of precious. She liked that he seemed at ease.

Finding herself enjoying the moment far too much, she broke the silence. "I remember one of my favorite places in the city is the Botanical Garden at Golden Gate Park. It's one of the most amazing places to me. But this is really nice, too."

They both looked at the violets and primroses mixed with an eruption of bluebells.

"Are there any special gardens in India?"

"Depends where in India. The climate is quite diverse there. It can be arid or tropical. The Taj Mahal has one of the more impressive gardens."

"I would love to visit the Taj Mahal. It must impressive to see it in person."

"It is."

"Have you ever taken your sister to India?"

He paused. "I haven't. Lucy's been to Europe a number of times, Japan once, and Australia. After our mother was diagnosed with breast cancer, we didn't travel much."

"I'm sorry. Was that fairly recent?"

"Five years ago. The cancer came back three years ago, and she died a year later. My father passed away last year. I think of a broken heart."

He was looking into the distance, and she couldn't read his expression.

"Seems like they were lucky to have such a loving marriage."

He turned to look at her. "Yes, they were."

"It must have been hard on you guys, especially your sister since she was much younger."

"Yes."

They walked across a bridge and fell into silence once more. Beyond the shrubs and a bed of rose bushes stood a little pavilion flanked by marble statues. On one side was a nude with his hand on his very stiff, very long cock. The other side was a female nude stretched on a pedestal, her mouth open, one hand gripping a sheet draped over half her body.

"Marguerite has a raunchy collection of art," Deana commented.

"You like it?"

She studied the statue of the man. A familiar sensation stirred in her groin. "I guess it's … titillating."

He grinned at her. She stepped up into the pavilion. When she turned and looked at him, his grin had faded, replaced by a serious expression.

"What is it?" she asked, wondering at first if he was troubled by concerns for his sister.

He sauntered to where she was. She saw then a ravenous look in his eyes, and her body responded immediately, her senses leaping to attention.

He tilted her chin up and ran his thumb against her lower lip. Her heartbeat quickened at his touch. She wondered that his ardor had been stirred so easily and that her own was proving every bit as eager.

CHAPTER 12

B ut his eyes also held a different look she couldn't place. His gaze traversed her face as if he were a scout surveying the terrain, landing eventually on her mouth. Lowering his head, he took her lips with his. Her guard melted away. Though they lacked complete privacy, she welcomed the kiss.

He worked her mouth with an almost tender quality, coaxing all sorts of feelings to stir inside of her, including that familiar longing in her abdomen. She detected the scent of his shaving cream mixed with the coffee he drank and idly realized that there was little about Rockwell that didn't appeal to her. She would've thought herself expended after the activities of last night, but she wanted him again.

"Should—we—return—to—the—house?" she asked in between his kisses.

"Why?" he murmured against her lips.

For privacy, of course. Instead, she replied, "You like public places."

His kisses became more adamant, more hungry. He held her head in place with one hand while he took whole mouthfuls of her. Instinctively she put a hand on his forearm, though he had yet to be very rough with her. Desire bloomed below her waist. He'd taken her last night. Would he go so far as to do that in the gardens?

As if in answer to her question, he abruptly swept her off her feet and laid her across the marble bench. He continued to kiss her, his tongue darting into her mouth only every so often, teasing her with the possibilities. She grew warm quickly, and not just from the heat of his body over hers. The simple weight of him on her was enthralling. She wasn't completely at ease with where they were, but she'd learned from her experience yesterday not to protest too much. And in truth her mind was being superseded by the wishes of her body.

The bench was cold and hard but another discomfort, one that could only be satisfied by him, proved more urgent. With every kiss on her neck, her collar, the tops of her breasts, the yearning grew. She arched her back, allowing him greater access to her neck. His hand was on one breast, pulling down her dress until he could access the nipple, which he sucked and fondled with his tongue. Arrows of desire shot from her breasts to her pussy, and she could feel the moisture gathering between her legs.

This was hardly fair. If she were to be publicly exposed in this way, the least he could do was to join her. She reached for the buttons of his jeans.

"Not yet," he mumbled as he placed her hands back at her sides.

After easing himself off of her, he pushed her skirt above her knees and spread them apart. Standing between her legs, he appraised her wanton position. She watched curiously as he lowered himself onto a knee. He kissed the inside of a thigh. She shivered at the delicate caress. His kisses trailed upwards to her cunt. His head was beneath her skirt.

"*Oh God,*" she mumbled when his tongue flicked at her clit.

Her body jumped, but he held her hips firmly in place.

"I can't," she protested, trying to sit up. This could be totally embarrassing if someone came.

"You will," he said from beneath her skirt.

She took a deep breath, squeezing her eyes shut when he licked her once more. Still unaccustomed to the touch, she attempted to squirm from his grasp.

"Relax and enjoy," he encouraged.

Reluctantly, she tried to settle down. He rubbed his tongue against her flesh.

"Ahhh!" she cried, jerking.

"Hold still," he commanded.

"I can't."

He looked up from under the skirt at her. "Are you defying me?"

She groaned, sensing defeat, but made a last attempt to defend herself. "Sorry, it's just … I thought someone was coming."

"No one's here."

With a sigh, she lay back, but he slapped the inside of her thigh with his hand, causing her to sit back up.

"What was that for?" she demanded.

"For stalling. Now, you will submit and, more importantly, you will come."

Impossible, she replied silently, but she lay back again. When he nuzzled her with his nose, it took all of her not to move. What if someone came on them, her legs spread, Rockwell going down on her?

He fondled her nub with his tongue. It was slick, and the sensation differed from his fingers. Moaning, she dug her nails into her palm. What if she didn't come? Would she be punished? Would she need to pretend?

"Oh!" she exclaimed when his tongue found a particularly sensitive spot.

It felt *delicious*. She concentrated on the sensations, pushing away thoughts of where it was happening. His touch became more forceful. Her resistance began to fade as he stoked her lust. She writhed on the rigid bench but didn't attempt to escape. Her legs, bent and exposed, felt awkward. The pressure in her built.

"God," she breathed when he sucked on her clit and tugged it gently with his teeth.

She was going to come. She should never have doubted him. He quickened his pace in response to her ascent. Tension, jarring and magnificent, mounted and spread from her sex into her abdomen and down through her legs. She almost feared the impending climax, wanting and resisting what was to come. He kept a firm grip on her hips and held her in place when, at last, the unraveling of her desire crashed through her body. Her legs flayed of their own accord, bumping against him, as the most magnificent shivers overcame her.

Her cry sent the birds scattering from the treetops. She felt as if she had been catapulted into the skies. When she sank back down from the heavens, her limbs a little weakened by the spasms, she found Rockwell on his feet, staring down at her. The area around his mouth and even his chin glistened from her moisture.

"Well done, Deana."

She flushed. "You're the one who did all the work."

He returned her smile and passed her his handkerchief. She applied it to his face first, admiring the contours of his lips as she wiped around it. Despite the exhibitionism of what he'd just done, she found his efforts endearing. Just as she'd finished cleansing his face, she realized he was staring at her with that unnamed intensity. She stared back, locked in his gaze. For several beats, the world consisted of only him and the beating of her heart.

As if startled, he put an end to the moment. "My turn."

He took the handkerchief from her and gently wiped the moisture that had dripped down her ass. He then offered her a hand up. Only then did she realize how relieved she was not to be lying against the marble. Just as her dress fell back down, they heard the sound of footsteps.

"Bella's awake," one of the female Chateau staff members told him.

"Did you let her know I wanted to talk?" he asked.

As the woman nodded, Deana willed herself not to be jealous.

He turned back to her. "I'll meet you at the library. Marguerite has an extensive collection of books and magazines."

"Are they as stimulating as her art?"

"You can be the judge of that," he replied with a grin.

"I'd like to stay in the garden."

"All right. I'll be back in about fifteen, twenty minutes."

She watched as he left, wondering what was so important that he had to leave her when they'd been in the middle of an intimate moment, all so he could speak to Bella. Was it Bella he was really interested in, and not her? It was none of her business, of course, and she had no intention of asking. She and Rockwell had no relationship or agreement beyond this weekend. The problem for her was that her feelings for Rockwell were growing. It was a disturbing development.

"Oooohhhh," Bella groaned as she held her head in her hands. She turned to the maid and snapped, "Close that curtain a bit. It's too bright in here."

Halsten handed Bella a cup of black coffee and pulled a chair alongside her bed where she lay propped against a mountain of pillows. "You shouldn't drink so much."

She glared at him, but as he remained unruffled, she turned her anger on the maid. "Stop scurrying around! Be still!"

"She'll be in bed for a while," he informed the maid. "Come back later."

Looking relieved, the maid left.

"Drink the coffee," he directed Bella.

She stared into the cup. "Will it cure my headache?"

"It'll help."

She took small sips.

"Have you reconsidered your stay here?"

"I can take care of myself."

"Your behavior doesn't instill me with confidence."

"Believe me, I have no intention of drinking so much again."

"I'll rest easy when you're home safe."

Her petulance faded and she looked at him with more appreciation. "You want to look after me?"

"Somebody has to. You're being careless and irresponsible."

She made an aggravated sound.

"I'm going to repeat what I said yesterday: you should stay away from Devon and Chateau Follet."

She shook her head and scowled. "Aren't you being hypocritical? You're here."

"I wouldn't have brought you here."

"What about Deana? You don't seem to have the same issues with her being here."

He felt unexpectedly angry that Bella was dragging Deana into the discussion. "Don't try to change the subject. We're talking about you."

"Have you tried to convince Deana to leave?" Bella pressed.

His conscience stirred uncomfortably. That the accusation of hypocrisy should come from an immature source made it no less true. "She's different."

"In what way?"

"You really want to go there?"

She grew quiet.

"Look, Bella, I'm not saying it's wrong for you to be interested in BDSM. Just don't try it with Devon. Not your first time."

"Are you suggesting you'd be better? If so, why didn't you ever bring it up when we were dating?"

"Because our relationship didn't make it far enough for me to try."

"Oh. So how long have you known Deana then?"

He took a breath to calm himself. Bella had always been stubborn. But her father had been a good man, had mentored Halsten and been there for him when his parents died. He owed it to her father to make sure Bella was safe, as he'd promised.

"It's not the same, and I'm not going to go into how it's different. My driver is staying here at the chateau. He can take you home."

"I don't want to go home. And Devon has been totally nice to me. I think you don't like him 'cause you're jealous."

It was all he could do not to roll his eyes. The conversation wasn't having the desired effect. He'd hoped to convince her to leave Chateau Follet, but Bella couldn't be reasoned with. And until he could rest easy about Bella, he couldn't devote all of his attention to Deana. And he very much wanted to. He wasn't sure why, but every minute he spent with her only made him want to spend another minute more.

Which meant he might never get enough of her.

CHAPTER 13

Halsten found Deana wandering the sculpture garden. He touched her back and she turned to him. She blushed. Her loveliness had somehow grown from a year ago. He wanted nothing more than to reach for her, but if he did, he was unsure he could stop himself from taking her on the pebbled ground. Or maybe he could pin her against a tree, her legs wrapped around him.

"How's Bella?" she asked.

"Hungover." He wouldn't tell her more. It was a delicate balance. He wanted Deana's support, even comfort, but Bella's business was her own; not his to share. Though he'd told Deana about Lucy, he knew his sister wouldn't mind his confidence in Deana, but Bella was another matter.

"Devon said he was going to check in on her."

His jaw clenched. "You saw him?"

"He was out here for a walk."

"What a coincidence."

"We chatted a little. He asked about my art and insisted on buying one of my watercolors."

Halsten tried to tame the jealousy that Devon had connected with her in a way he hadn't. "I didn't know you had art for sale."

"I don't officially. I had one piece shown in an art gallery years ago."

"I'd like to see some of your art. Do you have pics of them?"

"I have some on my phone, but I left my cell back in my room."

"Let's head back then."

He did want to see her art, but he also hoped to do more. He led her back to the path, hovering his hand over her lower back. She said nothing and neither did he. He admired the comfort of their silence. He knew far too many people who felt the need to fill a void with chatter.

Upstairs in the house, they had to pass by Bella's room to get to Deana's. They heard crying, and then a sharp slap.

Halsten pushed open the door to see Bella on her knees and Devon standing before her with his pants down.

Devon turned around. "What the fuck—"

"Are you okay?" Halsten asked Bella.

"Christ, I would have been fine if you wanted to watch. Just knock next time."

Halsten continued to stare at Bella, who nodded, though her eyes glistened with moisture.

"I—I was a bad girl," Bella murmured after wiping away some cum that clung to her bottom lip.

Halsten turned to Deana. "Why don't you go to your room."

Deana frowned but did as he suggested.

"She didn't swallow like I told her to," Devon explained as he zipped up his jeans.

"Mind if I talk to her alone?"

Devon folded his arms. "Why? Don't you have your own sub to look after?"

Halsten looked at Devon and imagined his fist in the guy's face. He turned to Bella. "Do you have a safeword?"

"What are you, her fucking nanny?"

"I'm fine, Halsten," Bella said, a little irritated.

He doubted she was fine. Was she trying to punish herself in her grief?

"This probably isn't the best place to be so soon after your father—"

"I'm *fine*. Jesus, Halsten."

"What about her father?" Devon asked.

"He passed away. Which makes Chateau Follet the perfect place to be because I need the distraction, okay?"

Halsten pressed his lips into a grim line. "I just don't want anyone to take advantage of you."

Devon balked. "Hey, I didn't know about her dad. And I wouldn't 'take advantage' anyway."

"Stop being so patronizing, Halsten," Bella added. "I'm not Lucille."

He sighed. "I'm here if you need anything."

"You take care of your sub, I'll take care of mine," Devon told him.

"This is Bella's first time here."

"Isn't it Deana's, too?" Bella asked.

Devon followed with his own question. "Yeah, shouldn't you be paying attention to her? Seems she's getting a little neglected."

Devon's words struck a chord. Halsten had noticed the look of disappointment on Deana's face when he'd asked her to go back to her room. Fighting Devon wouldn't help, though it would be satisfying. Nonetheless, the best strategy was to keep him away from Bella until one or the other could be removed entirely from the Chateau. Until then, what was he to do with Deana?

"Is something wrong?" Bhadra asked when she came to check on her.

Deana tried to smile and be polite. It wasn't Bhadra's fault that Rockwell was clearly interested in Bella and would be with her if it weren't for Devon and whatever obligation he might have felt to play the good host.

"I'm fine."

"Have you enjoyed your stay here?"

The woman's effort to initiate conversation surprised Deana out of her blues. "The hospitality has been more than welcoming."

There was a pause, and Deana wondered if Bhadra would protest that she hadn't intended to fish for compliments.

"And your company?" Bhadra continued. "With Mr. Rockwell?"

It was a direct question, and Deana wondered what prompted Bhadra to ask it. But she couldn't tell from Bhadra's impassive expression why she'd asked.

"Yes," Deana replied slowly. "You know, I wasn't too keen on him at first, but I've warmed up to him. But I think he'd rather be with Bella."

"Mr. Rockwell is most concerned with your welfare and asked me to treat you with the best of care."

"He's a good host."

"It's been some time since he was here, but in times past, it was apparent he only half-enjoyed his time and company."

Deana caught Bhadra's gaze for only a few seconds before she looked away. She wondered at the purpose of Bhadra's statement.

"But he seems very satisfied in yours," Bhadra finished.

Deana contemplated what had been said. Bhadra might know better than most the true sentiments of Rockwell. Perhaps he even confided in her. That he enjoyed his time with her, however, didn't negate his preference for Bella.

"Thank you, Bhadra," Deana acknowledged of the attempt to console her. "It's been nice to know you."

Bhadra gave a curt nod and showed Deana another outfit, including some sexy lingerie, she'd wear for dinner. Rockwell was generous, but why? Was he just going through the motions with her, as Bhadra implied that he had with others here? Deana looked at the reflection of herself in a pale blue dress. She wished there could be another night in which she could wear the sari. She'd felt beautiful then.

At dinner, Devon and Bella were absent. Though she had Rockwell all to herself, he seemed preoccupied and they barely spoke. Marguerite had card tables brought out after dinner. Deana encouraged Rockwell to play, thinking it might lighten his mood. They'd just sat down when Devon and Bella appeared. Contrary to her distracted state earlier, Bella now seemed in cheerful spirits. She flashed them a large smile as she walked in. Devon was his usual self.

"I might as well hand over my money now, right?" Devon quipped as the pair sat down at their table.

Deana raised a quizzical brow.

"Aren't you a master at card games?"

"Not all games," Deana replied, "and there's always the element of luck, which is never guaranteed."

"As there are four of us, maybe we should try something like whist."

"Whist?"

"I played it when I did a year at Oxford. It's basically like bridge."

Devon explained the gist of the game.

"Sounds fun," Deana said, then looked over at Rockwell, whose countenance had darkened considerably since the appearance of the couple.

"Let's do it then," Devon proclaimed with a large grin.

"What stakes shall we set?"

"Whatever you want," Bella replied. "Rockwell can afford anything."

Devon waved dismissively. "Playing for money is so basic. Let's do something more exciting."

Beside her, Rockwell stiffened. He seemed more displeased with Devon than ever.

"Like what?" she asked.

"If we win, you join us in the East Wing tonight. If you win, name your price."

Rockwell straightened as if interested. Deana wondered what he would name as the price. Would he ask for Bella? As for losing, venturing into the East Wing couldn't be so bad. After all, Bella was staying there.

"Why not?" Deana replied.

CHAPTER 14

Deana was conscious of Rockwell's stare but began shuffling. He put his hand on hers to stop her.

"I haven't agreed to the terms," he said.

"What's the matter, Halsten?" Bella asked. "You don't like our company or something?"

"Probably," Devon remarked, his own tone now serious and quite out of character.

Deana glanced between the two men. Had something happened between them?

"Or maybe he's worried," Devon continued, assuming his carefree manner again, "that his skills aren't up to par for the East Wing."

"What's required if we go in the East Wing?" Rockwell asked, his voice low and dark.

"That you mirror the activities."

Silence.

"No one's going to get hurt," Devon stated. "As you know, that's what safety words are for."

"The East Wing is quite exhilarating," Bella said to Deana.

"You shouldn't leave Chateau Follet without experiencing it for a night."

"I'd like to," Deana said. Though it may well ruin her stay at Follet, she wanted to force Rockwell's hand if they won.

"Come get a drink with me, Deana," Rockwell said rising to his feet.

She followed him over to the sideboard. She could tell he wasn't happy, but she couldn't determine who or what was the main culprit.

"I didn't give you permission to agree to Devon's terms," he said to her.

"You stated three rules in coming to Chateau Follet," she returned. "They had nothing to do with playing cards."

"I don't know what Devon has planned, but I'd trust a used car salesman over him."

"Then you have to win. If you want, I'll give you the option of naming the reward if we win."

He seemed to contemplate the enticement, then looked at her with searching eyes. "Are you sure you want to venture into the East Wing?"

She trembled with doubt, but she was assured in her speech. "I'm curious."

It was the truth, and if Bella could tolerate it, surely she could. They returned to the table.

"It seems I'm outvoted here," Rockwell said.

"Awesome!" Devon cried. "Let's begin."

Deana took a deep breath and handed the cards to Devon to shuffle. Rockwell then cut the cards. Her hands shook a little as she dealt the cards. To her surprise, Rockwell called to a servant for wine and poured them each a glass. Deana took a welcome sip and waited for Devon to play the first trick.

Devon and Bella won the first score, and Deana wondered if she'd been hasty in agreeing to the game. Despite her vast experience at cards, she didn't often play games with partnerships. Cards had become more of a vocation than a form of amusement for her, and it'd been some time since she'd played this game. Rockwell, however, appeared well versed in the game. In the next round, he won enough tricks to gain them two points. Then Rockwell and Deana, feeling more relaxed after finishing her wine, secured a third point. Devon and Bella won a point from the following hand to put themselves just one point behind Rockwell and Deana.

"This could go on all night!" Bella lamented.

"The partners to reach five points first wins," Rockwell explained.

They played two more hands and split the wins with one point per pair.

"I think I'd like to stretch my legs with a walk around the room," Deana said.

"Good idea!" Devon exclaimed.

"I need another drink," Bella said with a languid wave. "Halsten, would you?"

Rockwell seemed to hesitate between satisfying Bella's request or joining Deana and Devon.

"What would you like?" he asked Bella.

Of course, Deana sighed to herself and took Devon's arm.

"I gotta say," Devon began when they were out of earshot of anyone. "Halsten has all the luck. He's always here with some pretty, smart, and talented woman."

"Well, I'm not any of those," Deana replied, uncomfortable with his compliments.

"You sell yourself short, just as you don't charge enough for your art. You deserve more."

"You don't need to flatter me."

"I'm not. You're talented and under-appreciated." He shot a glance at Bella and Rockwell before turning his gaze back to her. "But tell me more about yourself. You're different from the women Rockwell usually brings here, and to be honest, I'm intrigued."

"As I was telling Bella at dinner last night, I'm not that interesting. There's very little to tell."

"A woman of mystery. That's even more intriguing!"

Observing his boyish grin and apparent sincerity, Deana could see how he could charm many women.

Devon leaned in toward her and lowered his voice. "You belong in the East Wing."

"What makes you say that?"

"I've known enough women in my lifetime. Got an internal radar for which ones are the more adventurous ones."

She gave him a dubious look, aware of Rockwell's unhappy gaze on them.

"You'll see that I'm right when we're in the East Wing."

"Are you that certain of winning?"

"I'm certain I haven't wanted anything more."

His stare bored into her, disconcerting her, and she suggested they not keep Rockwell and Bella waiting too much longer.

"Time to even the score," Devon said on sitting.

They executed exactly that and tied the score with four points per partnership. As the dealer in the next hand, Deana turned over a six of hearts for the trump card. Her heartbeat quickened. Hearts were not her favorite suit. For no rhyme or reason, she never had much luck with hearts. By this time, she was having second thoughts about whether or not she would do well with losing.

Rockwell took the first two tricks, then Devon, followed by Bella. Deana looked at Rockwell, who, as usual, was fairly expressionless when playing cards. She recalled how calm he'd been during that fateful hand when he possessed an ace and queen to best her king and ten.

Rockwell won the next trick, and Deana couldn't stop her heart from thumping. She wanted another glass of wine but no wish to ask permission for it in front of Devon and Bella. Eight tricks remained, and Devon took three of them in a row. Deana wondered if he'd been overly modest about his abilities at cards.

Deana won a trick, then Rockwell, then Bella.

"Now it's close," Devon said with a wicked gleam in his eyes.

"What would you claim if you win?" Bella asked of Rockwell, her gaze inviting as she peered over her cards at him.

Rockwell only smiled as he won the next trick. Two tricks remained, but Deana had a sinking feeling. Given the cards that she'd already observed and the two remaining in her hand—a paltry two of clubs and four of diamonds—unless Rockwell had two trumps remaining, their chances didn't look good.

Devon won the next trick. Deana saw the muscle along Rockwell's jaw tighten. The final suit was diamonds. Bella had no match. Rockwell had no match.

And Devon had a jack of hearts.

They were headed to the East Wing.

With a silent curse, Halsten watched as a smile spread from ear to ear on Devon's face. Halsten had nothing against taking Deana there. Frankly, he would've liked nothing more. But she hadn't been at Chateau Follet for long. And he would've wanted her there on his own terms.

"Well played," Devon complimented Deana. "Don't be discouraged, Deana. As you say, there's the element of luck. It's not always about skill."

He finished off his glass of wine. "Now then, shall we start the night right?"

Halsten had studied Bella throughout the game. She'd shown none of the hesitancy or reserve from the afternoon. He wondered at her change. He looked next to Deana, who didn't seem as confident as she was earlier. He'd allowed her a glass of wine to calm her nerves and contemplated another glass for her. He'd ensure her safety, but she may well need the additional support.

He shouldn't have placed her in such a position. The enticement to name the prize should they have won was too much. He knew exactly what he would've asked for: Devon to leave Chateau Follet as soon as possible.

"I have the perfect room in mind," Devon said and practically skipped out of the drawing room and into the hallway.

Rockwell clenched his jaw but followed the man with Deana beside him.

"Have you explained to Bella what she may expect in the East Wing?" he asked Devon.

"She's seen for herself," Devon replied.

"You're so funny, Halsten," Bella said, glancing back at him. "I'm not your little sister Lucille."

They were in the East Wing, and the art soon reflected the kinkier nature of the activities there. Whereas the West Wing was adorned with nudes or paintings of a man and a woman in various positions of copulation, the same nudes held whips and chains in the East Wing, and paintings of couples were often engaged in *ménage-a-trois*. One such painting featured a woman penetrated by two men with disproportionately large cocks. Rockwell noticed Deana's eyes widening as she realized that one of the cocks was inserted in the woman's ass. She turned red and tightened her grip on his arm.

"We won't do anything you don't want to."

She seemed to believe him, but he couldn't tell if she were comforted by the fact.

"I had this room specially reserved," Devon announced as he paused in front of a set of gilded double-doors.

He pushed one of the doors opened, bowed and swept his arm. "Ladies first."

Bella entered and gasped. Miss Herwood followed and paused briefly in her tracks.

Unlike the ornate set of doors that led to it, the chamber was sparse and austere. No silk wallpaper or golden candelabras adorned the walls, no carpeting or rugs to cover the cold, dull floor. The only furnishing comprised two beds on either side of the room, facing each other. The head and foot boards were made of wrought iron more appropriate for a dungeon cell. On them dangled chain shackles. Only plain white sheets covered the mattresses. Along the back wall hung all manner of instruments: canes, crops, whips, and more. On the shelves were additional accessories of pain and pleasure. A fire had been started in the stone hearth, casting eerie shadows throughout the room.

"You sure this is the right room?" Bella asked.

"Definitely," Devon murmured as he appraised the room, the glow of lust already lighting his face.

Halsten eyed Deana. She wasn't entirely new to such a spectacle, but Devon's room was far more grim than she must've expected.

"Now then, the first order of business: I think the women are wearing far too much!" Devon declared.

"The first order of business in the East Wing is always to establish the safeword," Rockwell corrected, his patience tested already.

"How about 'cease and desist'?"

"A single word is easier to remember, one that's not subtle but obvious."

Devon rolled his eyes. "It can be Humpty Dumpty for all I care."

"A *single* word."

Halsten wanted to wring the man's neck. It was proving to be a long night already.

"Scotland," Bella suggested. "I'm traveling there with my aunt and uncle later this year."

"Does that work for everyone?"

Deana nodded.

"Now, let's start!" Devon said. He staked a claim on his side of the room and pulled Bella to him.

Devon reached for the zipper on her dress.

"Is there no curtain? After all, they can *see*," Bella said.

"That's the point. And we can see them." He eyed Deana in a way that made Halsten's blood simmer with anger. "It'll heighten the experience, I guarantee it."

Halsten frowned. Devon was the last person he wanted to share a room in the East Wing with.

Deana walked carefully to the other side of the room. She looked around her. Was she seeking a means of escape or a place to hide? Seeing none, she seemed to steel herself. Devon had Bella's dress undone and was moving to her lingerie.

"Remember you can say the safeword at any time," Halsten reminded Deana.

She nodded and slipped out of her shoes.

He inhaled sharply. Her acquiescence meant more to him than he expected. He undid her dress. He waited, but she said nothing. Across the room, Bella giggled as Devon tossed her garment away with flourish.

Slowly, Halsten slid the dress from Deana's shoulders. She kept her eyes downcast. It fell to the floor, leaving her in her underwear, stockings and garters. Having engaged in a *ménage-a-trois* before, he was no stranger to sharing a woman. But he had no desire to share Deana—with anyone, let alone Devon. Looking across the room, he found Devon eyeing Deana again. Halsten would've done almost anything to bring pleasure to Deana, but at the moment he wanted nothing more than for her to utter the safeword and put an end to their situation.

Bella, in a similar state of undress, glanced over to them. A small smile graced her colored lips, maybe from believing she was more appealing than Deana. Seeing Halsten's gaze, Devon smirked and ran both hands down Bella's pale, bare arms.

Halsten returned his attention to Deana. Devon could believe whatever he wished, Halsten knew he had the better woman. He waited until Devon began undoing Bella's garters before doing the same. Deana trembled slightly as he pulled at the clips.

"Do you need the safeword?" he whispered in her ear.

She shook her head.

"Are you cold?"

"No."

With a deep breath, he removed her stockings. Any moment now she'd be completely naked; naked before that son of a bitch Devon.

But despite his loathing of their situation, the ability of her beautiful body to arouse Halsten persevered. His groin tightened.

Bella cried out and giggled as Devon, aroused and impatient, stripped her stockings away too quickly, ripping the delicate nylon.

"More than just eye candy, am I right, Rockwell?" Devon declared.

Bella attempted some modesty and covered her breasts with her arms, but Devon tore her arms away. Her shapely breasts, vaguely marked on the sides by the boning of her bustier, stood at smart attention. Her rosy areolas constricted as her nipples hardened.

"Your turn, Rockwell."

Deana stiffened and he wondered if his own discomfort was contagious. Maybe she'd do better if he took a different approach and helped put her more at ease through arousal. He might be able to teach Devon, through demonstration, how better to handle a woman, how to attend to her pleasure.

Halsten slid his hand down her shoulders and planted a soft kiss on her left shoulder. He ran his fingers across her collarbone, then gripped the back of her neck, and tried to massage away the tension. Her head dropped lower, and he could feel her tightness loosen a little. Gently, he undid her bra and pulled it down her arms, exposing her breasts.

Devon drank her in. "Sweet, right?"

Halsten shot him a look to indicate he wasn't interested in talking to the man.

Devon reached both hands around Bella and tweaked her nipples. Bella squealed.

Halsten held each of Deana's breasts in his hands and planted a reverential kiss on one, then the other. He ran his thumbs over the nipples. They peaked in response to his touch.

"These are a lovely sight," he murmured. "Finer than a Titian or a Reuben."

He lifted one breast and tugged on the nipple with his mouth. He sensed her breathing become uneven. Her pupils had dilated, and the whites of her eyes had a shimmer.

Good. She was adjusting.

He pulled her naked body to him and took her mouth. One hand slid to cup her buttocks. She felt divine even through his clothes. From the corner of his gaze, he saw Devon do the same with Bella. But instead of a choreographed dance of the lips and tongue, Devon mauled Bella's mouth, smearing her lipstick and causing the flesh around her mouth to flush as if she had a rash.

Halsten pushed his fingers through Deana's hair and manipulated her head to taste her mouth from different angles. He had wondered how aroused he could be while occupying a room with a man he detested, but he could easily be consumed by Deana, his awareness of Devon repressed by his own growing lust.

"Care to exchange partners?" Devon asked.

"What?" Bella asked. "You didn't say anything about that."

Devon slapped her across the face. Bella looked shocked, and Deana, who had avoided looking toward the other side of the room, glanced over sharply. Halsten clenched a first.

"I didn't say you could talk."

A contrite Bella looked down at her feet.

"Your safeword can be used at any moment," Halsten told her, earning a glare from Devon. He clenched his teeth and said to him, "No exchange. Have you reviewed the rules?"

Devon waved a hand dismissively. "She'll learn. We're consenting adults. The element of surprise is exciting."

Devon looked over at Deana, who quickly glanced away. Her reaction incited the man to walk over to her. He circled her like a vulture over a carcass. Halsten felt every muscle in his body tense. If the ass-wipe touched her in the slightest, he'd punch the man.

"Nice," Devon smirked before returning to his side of the room. He pinched at Bella's nipples. "I think these need a little decoration."

He went over to a shelf and retrieved a pair of small clamps with weights dangling by small metal chains.

"Has she worn them before?" Halsten interrupted. "If not, she shouldn't start with the weighted clamps."

Both the women had eyes wide.

"Weights make it a lot more fun," Devon returned.

"Do you remember the safeword?" Halsten demanded of the women.

They both nodded.

"You're not chickening out, are you?" Devon pressed. "If you don't have what it takes and want to welch on a bet ..."

With a silent oath, Halsten grabbed Deana from behind, pressed her to him, and reached for her clit. To apply the nipple clamps so soon to a novice without arousing her first was cruel. He rubbed her between the legs. It took longer as Deana wasn't completely at ease still with the lack of privacy, but she eventually began to pant softly and squirm against him. Devon watched with amusement. Halsten weighed the prospect of stopping and beating up the man, but then Devon might press charges. Halsten's first responsibility was to Lucy.

"Since you've done such a fine job stimulating her, I think your slut should be the first to try these," Devon said, offering the pair of clamps to Halsten.

Reluctantly, he took the clamps from Devon. No state of arousal would take away the bite.

"These will hurt," he informed her. "Do you wish to continue?"

Deana nodded. He pinched the clamps open and applied them to the nipples as lightly as he could while still holding the weights. She gasped when he released the clamps. He waited for her to utter the safeword, but she didn't.

"Breathe," he told her. "Gently."

She followed his instruction and tried to moderate her breathing. When he saw the pain had settled, he slowly removed his hand from the weight. Her eyes widened as the weight pulled her nipples down.

"Oh God," she mumbled.

He searched her face. Even with the safeword, the pain could be too great. She let out a few haggard breaths, then looked at him with clear eyes. He appraised her appearance and instantly felt his blood warm. The adornments looked fucking amazing on her.

"Well done," Devon praised.

Bella had watched with intense curiosity and frowned at the compliment paid to Deana. Devon retrieved another pair and affixed a clamp to her nipple. She screamed and choked back a sob. Halsten noted her eyes watering. But she appeared determined to bear it at least as well as Deana. Devon applied the other clamp and stepped back to admire the result.

"Stand straight," Devon told Bella.

Bella bit down on her lower lip and attempted to do as he said.

"The clamps shouldn't stay too long," Halsten recommended. "They need proper training."

Devon poked at one of the weights to make it sway.

"Ah, ah, ah," cried Bella.

Devon grinned. "Imagine how they'd swing if we applied a flogger at the same time!"

Ignoring Devon, Halsten cupped Deana's chin and kissed her.

"You are so sexy and strong," he murmured against her lips.

His hand went between her legs to fondle her there, and he was relieved to feel her wetness coating his fingers.

"Take these off, please," Bella begged. "Please!"

"But you just got them on," Devon replied.

"Let's move on," Halsten suggested. Whatever anger he felt toward Bella for her behavior, he didn't want to see her in pain, as she already must be from her grief.

"Fine," Devon acquiesced. He removed the nipple clamps to Bella's immense relief. "Now on your knees, whores!"

CHAPTER 15

Thank heaven, Deana thought to herself when Rockwell removed the clamps. Her poor nipples would be tender for some time. Despite the piercing pain of having the damn things clipped to her, however, her body had still responded to the man's touch. She was grateful to be with Rockwell and not Devon.

"On your knees!" Devon reiterated.

Bella and Deana exchanged glances before complying. For the first time, Deana felt on some common ground with Bella.

Devon situated his pelvis before Bella and rubbed his crotch. "I think we deserve some attention."

He unbuttoned his trousers and pulled out his cock. Bella gaped at the length of the curved erection.

"Open your mouth."

"You want me to—" she began until he slapped her once more.

"Dirty whores love to suck cock, right? Especially big ones like mine."

Deana nearly rolled her eyes, though he may have a point as to the length. She was glad Rockwell's wasn't that long—but it was glorious, filling her like no one else had.

Bella opened her mouth a little. He shoved himself into the opening. She recoiled, but he had his hand at the back of her head. She gagged and flayed.

"Try your best to relax," Rockwell said.

After struggling with the abrupt intrusion into her mouth, Bella managed to calm her reflexes. Devon pulled her head to and fro so that her mouth moved up and down his shaft. Occasionally, she appeared to choke when he pushed himself too far into her mouth.

"Why are you hesitating?" Devon asked Rockwell with a pointed look at his crotch.

Rockwell frowned for the hundredth time at Devon before unbuttoning his own pants. Deana had seen his cock before but not at such an intimate distance. Like Bella, she stared at the appendage with its bulbous head and rigid veins. She, possibly like Bella, wasn't much for giving blow jobs. She looked into his eyes. His pupils seemed to have melted.

She parted her lips. He took the invitation and inserted the top of his cock. She tasted a drop of saltiness upon her tongue. He eased more of himself into her mouth. He was so hard it made her pussy clench. She wrapped her lips closely around him and thought she heard him groan. He closed his eyes. Reveling in her ability to have such an effect on him, she attempted to take more of his cock. But when it reached her throat, she, too, gagged. He retracted himself. Wanting to try again, she grabbed his cock and guided it into her mouth once more. Surprised, he allowed her. She was surprised too, that she wanted to please him in this way.

"Yes, yes!" Devon cried as he bucked his hips at Bella. "Eat it good!"

Deana attempted to glide her mouth in a similar manner up and down Rockwell's erection. Eventually she found a rhythm, cradling him on her tongue. She liked the sound of him groaning as he eased himself further into her.

"God, that feels good," he grunted, fisting his hand into her hair.

On the other side of the room, Devon growled as he began to come. Bella appeared to retch. Halfway through, he pulled out his cock and sprayed the remainder of his cum over her face. A bit found its way into her hair. Devon stumbled backwards, shaking his head.

Deana looked at Rockwell, wondering if the same end would come to her. But Rockwell pulled himself out completely. She couldn't help her disappointment. She wanted to bring him to orgasm.

"Now that's what I'm talking about," Devon said to Bella. After collecting himself, he looked over at Rockwell. "Problem?"

"I can wait," Rockwell responded evenly.

"Can't run more than one race?"

Rockwell made no reply.

"See there? Mine is hardening again already," Devon said as he fondled himself.

"You have a need to impress me?" Rockwell asked.

Devon rolled his eyes, then turned his attention to the bed. He patted the mattress. "Up here, whore."

Wiping at her face, Bella made her way to the bed. Devon had her face the footboard and applied a pair of short shackles to her wrists. They pulled her down and made her look as if she were embracing the mattress. He lifted her hips so that she was on her knees, her ass high in the air. Devon began to shed his clothes.

While Halsten pulled off his shirt, Deana went to assume the same position on the bed. Earlier she had avoided gazing at the other couple, but now she felt a little transfixed at seeing them. There was undoubtedly an arousing quality at witnessing others, a quality that was both uncomfortable and titillating. Rockwell certainly looked over frequently, but was it because he found stimulation from being a spectator or was it Bella that drew his gaze? She was as gorgeous nude as she was clothed.

Deana was able to glimpse and admire the naked form of Rockwell before he applied similar shackles to her wrists. Pinned to the bed, she could do little more than shift her head from side to side. He lifted her hips, and her pussy tingled in anticipation.

Devon had walked over to the wall and found two wooden paddles. He tossed one to Rockwell.

"Let's make their asses red."

Bella began to whimper.

Deana twisted her head and could barely make out Devon and Bella from the corners of her eyes. She felt the bed sink with Rockwell's weight. He was kneeling behind her. Once more she felt his hand between her legs. With a delighted moan, she parted her legs further to allow him full access. He fondled her clit, coaxing from her that clear honey of desire. With his other hand, he caressed the curve of her ass. He swatted one cheek. His next blow landed a little heavier, but nothing to make her jump. She was more engrossed in the delightful sensations being generated between her legs. He strummed her clit while pressing his thumb on a raised and sensitive area inside of her. Wonderful, agonizing tension flared deep and hot inside of her.

Whap!

Devon had applied the paddle to Bella, who screamed. Both Rockwell and Deana stilled.

Whap!

Another scream.

The paddle was thicker and harder than the tails of a flogger, Deana considered. Rockwell resumed his fondling, and she forgot her concerns. Would he let her come? Could she orgasm before witnesses?

Yes, oh yes, she answered herself when his ministrations intensified. He slapped her ass with his hand. The bright sting felt delicious. Awash in that tangled mix of pain and pleasure, she felt her ascent looming.

But then he let fall the paddle, and she heard her own scream.

The pain was large and penetrating. She heard a steady rain of slaps from the other side of the room.

"Stop! Please stop!" Bella cried. "Ah!"

Deana hoped Bella screamed for effect. She hoped Bella remembered the safeword.

The paddle struck the bottom of her own buttock, and Deana gritted her teeth. Rockwell attended to her pussy once more. Moaning, she reveled in his skills as he took her body through that blissful craving. The sounds from the other side of the room blurred with her increased desire, her increased need for release. He rubbed her more intensely, making her toes curl. She prayed he wouldn't stop. Her cries became ones of urgency and anticipation.

But just as she approached the precipice, he withdrew his hand and once more applied the paddle. It smarted, but she was more intent on her release. She pushed her cunt at him, wanting him to finish the job. He spanked her once more with the paddle.

"Ah! Please ..." she groaned.

On the other side of the room, Devon discarded the paddle and lay on his back, his head between Bella's thighs. He pulled her pussy down to his face.

Bella looked as if her eyes might pop from their sockets, but then her eyelids lowered as she realized the pleasure from Devon's efforts. Deana and Rockwell both paused to observe her.

"Yes, yes, yes!" Bella cried, then shuddered as paroxysms of ecstasy overcame her.

Filled with envy, Deana implored Rockwell to continue, arching her back and pushing her backside toward him.

"Are you offering your ass or your pussy?" he asked in response to her movements.

"Please finish," she murmured.

He caressed her sodden flesh, then buried his cock inside of her.

Yes! Her pussy took him in hungrily. He sank the full length of his cock into her. She closed her eyes and marveled at the fullness between her legs. Circling an arm around her hip, he played with her clit. It didn't take long for her to come undone. His thick, hard rod filling her combined with the stimulation of her clit shot her over the precipice. She shattered into spasms, losing all control of her limbs.

She had yet to recover when he began his next assault. He bucked against her, holding her up by the waist. His scrotum slapped against her nether lips. She felt the hair at his groin against her ass as he drove himself deep inside of her. At first there was some discomfort as her first wave receded, blocked in part by another coming wave. As the second grew in size, she felt herself awash once more. His cock pommeled into her with increasing speed.

"Oh my God!" she screamed.

Her body crashed into the heavens. All else became nothing.

When Deana settled back down, she became vaguely aware that Rockwell had pulled out of her. Her legs had buckled under her and she lay prone on the bed. She heard panting and grunting from the other side of the room. Prying open her eyes, she saw Devon buried inside Bella, pounding her into the mattress. With a howl, Devon found his release and collapsed onto the bed.

Rockwell got off the bed, and Deana saw his cock was still stiff. Why had he not pushed himself to orgasm? Did he find her unsatisfactory somehow? Did he not want to impose on her now that she'd finished? Or was he somehow saving himself for Bella? She watched Rockwell approach Bella and release the shackles from her wrists. She turned onto her side and lay beside Devon.

Returning, Rockwell then removed the shackles form Deana.

She sat up and rubbed her wrists as Rockwell gathered his clothes. He stepped into his pants and pulled on his shirt. Assisting her off the bed, he helped her dress. He looked over at Bella and Devon, who'd begun to snore in his sleep.

"We've fulfilled our bet," Rockwell told her.

She hoped he meant only the one with Devon and Bella, and not that he was done with her. They left the room and headed back to the West Wing.

They walked the rest of the way in silence. Rockwell appeared grim. He must not have enjoyed himself. She supposed it was unpleasant to watch another man with the woman he wanted for himself.

"Maybe we shouldn't have played cards," she said as they approached her room.

He looked at her sharply. "I'm sorry you had to endure the consequences."

"No regrets. I wanted to experience the East Wing. It was … arousing and thrilling." He seemed relieved. "I only meant that you didn't seem to enjoy it."

"If you liked it, Deana, then I did. How's your ass?"

"I may spend most of tomorrow standing up."

He grinned. "Maybe you'll think twice before ever accepting a proposition from Devon."

"It seems I'm prone to accepting improper propositions."

His gaze bored into her, and without warning, he pinned her against the door with his body. His mouth descended on hers, engulfing her yelp of surprise. He raised both her arms above her, locking her head in position as he devoured her. She could barely catch a breath, and for the moment, she didn't care that he wanted Bella. He was with her, and she would satisfy him.

She attempted to return his kiss, but he was too much in command, too hungry. She felt the hardness of his desire against her and arched her back, pushing herself further into him. He opened the door, and they tumbled into the darkened room. She fell on top of him, their lips still joined. His left hand cradled her head while his right hand grasped a buttock firmly. She ground herself against his erection.

They kissed as if searching for something within the other to satiate their appetites. Her head spun from the effort to keep up with his forceful exertions. He rolled her under him and moved the one hand from her head to a breast. He gained access to her nipple. He pinched it gently through her garments. She cried out as the nipple was still sensitive from the clamps.

With a groan, he pulled her up, swept her off her feet, and deposited her on the bed. Her hands made quick work of his shirt and pants. Remembering his look when she'd had him in her mouth, she encased his cock once more and sucked hard. She tried to take in as much of him as she could, but his length made her gag when he hit the back of her throat. Forcing herself to relax, she made an attempt with better success. Rockwell emitted an oath and undulated his hips, pushing his cock in and out of her mouth.

He pulled her head away. "You'll make me come."

She stared at him. "I know."

Shaking his head, he pushed her into the bed and turned her on her stomach to access the zipper on her dress. Soon he had her stripped naked once more and on her back. His hands roamed over her body, kneading breasts, gripping hips, and squeezing her buttocks before finding their way between her legs. Still wet from before, she was slippery to the touch. She enjoyed his caresses there, but she wanted him in a deeper way.

"Take me," she said in a husky voice beside his ear.

He looked into her eyes as if contemplating the invitation, then slid off the bed. He pulled her to the edge of the bed and spread her thighs wide. His thumb strummed her clit, heating the familiar sensations of delight and agitation.

"Do it," she implored.

"As you wish," he replied, pointing his cock at her cunt and driving it into her.

Feeling victorious, she willed the muscles in her pussy to grab at him.

"God," he breathed as he buried himself further into her.

She savored the fullness inside of her before beginning a slow grind of her hips. Propped above her, he buried his face in the crook of her neck as he moved his lower body in rhythm, thrusting in and out. He mouthed her neck and planted kisses along her shoulder. She arched her back and jerked herself harder against him. He responded by pushing himself up off of her and tossing her ankles over his shoulders. Wrapping an arm around her legs to hold them in place, he shoved his cock deep into her.

"Oh!" she cried as he buried himself to the hilt.

The penetration struck new areas within her.

"Harder," she instructed.

He withdrew, then rammed himself back in.

"Ah!"

He repeated several times until she clutched the sheets beneath her. Her climax began to build. He quickened his pace. She marveled that he could exhibit such force from this part of his body. The bed shook and creaked from their actions. Her breasts bounded up and down.

As her ecstasy loomed, she wondered if she could ever be with any other man. Her abdomen clenched as divine sensations ricocheted wildly inside of her. Her body could no longer contain them. She screamed as they raked through her.

He shoved himself at her, his cock seeking her womb. She felt something hot spilling into her. He shuddered, then bucked his hips against her a few more times. Perspiration glistened on his brow. After withdrawing, he collapsed onto the bed beside her, his breathing hard. She pulled her legs onto the bed.

"Thank you," she murmured.

She felt spent but triumphant. He wrapped an arm around her and pulled her to him.

"Chateau Follet suits you well, Deana," he replied.

CHAPTER 16

"*Votre Mademoiselle est si jolie,*" Marguerite remarked to Halsten, who stood overlooking the grounds from the veranda where the lady of the house was hosting morning tea for several guests.

He turned to look where Deana sat at the table. The sun had found its way through the clouds at that moment. Deana seemed to radiate the rays that shone on her. Her eyes sparkled with uncommon brightness and her cheeks bore a natural flush. When he'd first spotted her in the club over a year ago, he'd barely given her a second look, but the more he observed of her, the more she intrigued him. This morning, he thought her uniquely beautiful.

In many ways, he wanted to forget as much of last night as possible. The vision of Devon on top of Bella would make him cringe for years to come. But there were moments he would come back to over and over again. Surprisingly, one of those moments was when he held Deana in his arms while she slept, listening to the rhythm of her breath, feeling it on his chest.

As if sensing his gaze on her, Deana looked up and smiled at him over her teacup. He felt his heart swell and would return her smile, but Devon appeared.

"Jesus, it's bright out here," he grumbled.

Halsten felt his jaw tighten as he watched Devon. Deana, possibly recalling the events of last night, shifted in discomfort and placed her attention on her tea.

"Morning," Devon noted to her, "Sleep well after our activities last night?"

Halsten went to stand near Deana.

"Morning to you, too, Halsten," Devon smirked.

"Where's Bella?" Halsten asked.

"Still getting ready, probably. It probably takes her an hour just to put on her makeup." He turned to Deana. "Is that how long it takes you?"

"I really just apply liptstick, so it doesn't take me long," she replied.

Halsten was glad to see that she didn't seem too interested in conversing with Devon, who stretched out his legs and arms.

"So you saw Bella this morning?" Halsten asked.

"Yep," Devon replied with what seemed to Halsten a smug expression.

Halsten felt uneasy. He didn't want to leave Deana with Devon but he felt the need to check on Bella.

"I'm going to—I'll be back in a few minutes," he said to Deana. He then returned to Marguerite. "Can you keep an eye on Deana? Make sure she's safe from Devon."

Marguerite smiled. "Protective or jealous?"

Halsten didn't respond. She put a hand on his arm. "Don't worry. I'll do what you ask."

He made his way to Bella's room. He heard sniffling from behind the door before he knocked.

"Go away," Bella replied.

"It's me, Halsten."

"Go away."

"Are you okay?"

"What part of 'go away' don't you understand?"

She wasn't okay. He tried the doorknob. Opening the door, he found Bella in her bed, wearing a sexy babydoll nightie, a tissue in her hand. Her eyes appeared moist and faintly red and puffy.

"What happened?" he demanded.

"What are you, like, my father?"

"Devon said he was just here, so that means there's a high chance nothing good happened."

She sniffed. "It's none of your business anyway. You've got that Deana girl. Where is she?"

Halsten put his hands on his hips. "You look like you've been crying. Did Devon do something to you?"

"God, you're nosy."

"What did he do?"

She rolled her eyes. "We had sex, okay? Isn't that what this place is all about?"

"Did he hurt you?"

"Do you really care?"

He clenched his hand. Dealing with Lucy might be easier than dealing with Bella. "Of course I care."

"You seemed more interested in Deana last night."

"I'm sorry you felt that way. It wasn't the case. Now answer my question: did Devon hurt you? Did he assault you?"

Her bottom lip quivered but she said, "No."

"I don't buy it."

"We had anal sex, okay? It was my first time, and I didn't know it was going to hurt so much."

"Did you want to have anal sex?"

"Not exactly, but I didn't say no. He said it would be more amazing than regular sex."

He ran a hand through his hair. Even if Bella had given her unequivocal consent, he'd punch Devon just for the hell of it if the guy was standing here right now.

"I didn't say no," she added, "so it's not like he raped me or anything."

"What did you say?"

"Nothing. I didn't say anything."

"Did you guys have a safeword?"

"He didn't mention it, but maybe he figured it was the same one as last night."

He shook his head. "Why are you defending the guy? "

All of a sudden, Bella burst into tears. "I don't know. It just feels like I'm to blame."

Putting aside his anger, Halsten went over to Bella and wrapped an arm about her, holding her until her cries subsided.

"We should get you home, Bella," he said softly as she continued to tremble.

"I don't know ..."

As he wondered what else he could say to persuade her, he spotted a pill bottle on the bedside table. He picked it up. Klonopin. But it wasn't her name on the bottle. "Where did you get this?"

"Jenny Sanders. I think you met her once or twice. She was my roommate back at USC."

"You're taking someone else's medication?"

"She said it really helped her with her anxiety."

"You can't go around self-medicating yourself, Bella. You should see a doctor and get evaluated for your own prescription."

She grabbed the pill bottle from him. "I don't need to see a psychiatrist."

"My driver can take you home."

"I don't want your driver ... But *you* can take me home."

He frowned. He couldn't leave Deana at the Chateau.

As if sensing his thoughts, Bella pronounced, "I'm not going home alone, so if you're not going to take me, I'll stay."

"With Devon?" He asked, his anger rising again.

She picked up the imaginary lint on her nightie. "Maybe I'll meet someone else."

He sighed. He didn't like having his hand forced this way, but

Bella needed help. "All right. I'll take you home, but I need to check in with Deana first."

"Leaving? Today?" Deana echoed as she turned to look at Rockwell standing in the doorway to her chamber with his hands behind him.

"Bhadra would accompany you if you like."

"I like Bhadra, but I don't need a babysitter. What about you?"

"I have to take Bella home. She needs someone to look after her."

That explained it, Deana thought to herself wryly.

"But if you want to stay, I'll honor my duty as your host."

She frowned. He saw her as his duty?

"And as far as I'm concerned, you've fulfilled your end of our deal," he said. "I'll have the balance wired to your account today."

"Thank you."

She pretended to study the contents of the vanity, too consumed with a rush of sadness to look at him. She hadn't anticipated their time would come to this abrupt end, but she didn't want to keep him from Bella. Why shouldn't she leave? So that she could enjoy his company for one more day? To what end? Parting ways was the wiser course of action, for them both.

When she felt she had mastery over her feelings, she said, "Whatever works for you."

He seemed relieved, and she knew then she'd made the right decision. He approached her and held out a box he'd been holding behind him.

"I want you to have these."

Opening the lid, he revealed the Indian jewelry she'd worn the other day. Her eyes lighted at the sight of the exquisite baubles, but she knew she couldn't accept.

"I had to sell your last gift," she said, embarrassed. "These are too nice for such a sad fate."

"Then keep them."

She would've, but she needed no reminders of him. "I don't need anything more beyond what we've already agreed to."

To her surprise, he appeared hurt.

"You've been generous enough, and I actually enjoyed my time here."

Her words seemed to cheer him. "You're quite a woman."

She smiled. He stared at her intensely. She withdrew her hand.

"I should get packing," she said, hoping he'd leave before her composure vanished.

He gave a curt nod, turned and left. Deana stared at the closed door for several minutes.

Dammit. She missed him already.

CHAPTER 17

Halsten hadn't realized he had been staring out the car window until Bella pressed her leg against his.

"So, you ever had anal sex before?" She asked.

He glanced briefly at her, replying, "Yes."

"Is it really more amazing than regular sex?"

"For some, it can be. So Devon didn't know he was hurting you?"

He wouldn't put it past the fucker not to care.

Bella pouted, "I don't want to talk about him. Did the women you had anal sex with like it?"

"They said they did, but it's not for everyone, and they weren't anal virgins at the time."

Bella thought for a moment. "Maybe I'd be willing to give it another shot."

She slid her leg along his.

"Bella, I'm taking you home because I don't think being at Chateau Follet is healthy for you right now."

"Fine, I agree. I'd rather do something at my place ... Or here in the car."

He frowned. "Bella, I just want to see you safely home."

"That sounds super boring."

He returned to looking out the window.

"You didn't used to be this boring," she said.

"People change."

As if realizing he wasn't going to say anything more, she sat back in her seat and crossed her arms in front of her. "Guess so."

The rest of the ride was fairly silent. Bella texted on her phone, checked out some Instagram videos, then took a nap. He saw her into her condominium. She made one last attempt to flirt with him, and when it was clear he wasn't receptive, she couldn't seem to get rid of him soon enough, though he had offered to get some food for the both of them.

Back in his car, he called a mutual friend to check in on her, then sat back in silent thought for several minutes before deciding to call Deana.

"Well?"

Halsten pulled his gaze from the wall and turned to the lovely young woman seated to his left at the breakfast table. Lucille had dark hair, a petite frame, and large, round, innocent eyes that she used to great effect on most people.

His sister scowled. "Didn't you hear a word I said?"

"No," he admitted.

He could smell the Darjeeling tea at the table. The scent reminded him of India. And Deana. Once he'd gotten Bella the help she needed, he'd thought of little else since departing Chateau Follet, though he'd thought his time there would satiate and purge his need for her. He could fool himself into thinking it was because he'd failed to spend that third and final night with her, but his passion for her had only grown. If anything, his shortened time had saved him from becoming irretrievably enamored.

What stopped him was the lack of reciprocity. She had a physical attraction to him. That much he was sure. It seemed like Deana had a pragmatism that allowed her to separate physical desire from the heart. She'd given no indication that she wanted anything more than their *business* arrangement. He'd given her the opportunity to have that final night together, and she'd declined. Maybe she was just being nice, but she didn't say or do anything that suggested she wanted a third night at Chateau Follet. She'd even refused his gift of the jewelry. He had called her after dropping off Bella and left a message when she didn't answer, but she hadn't called him back. He had called her once more, but she hadn't answered then either.

"Hal, do I have to ask a *third* time?"

"I'm sorry," he said with a concerted effort to hear what Lucy had to say.

She narrowed her eyes. "What's with you? Are you feeling okay?"

"Please ask your question, and for the last time, I promise."

"Are you going to let me go or are you going to be the tyrant again?"

He smiled. "I don't have any problems with being a tyrant."

"How long are you going to dictate my life?"

"Are we talking about Mexico again?"

"No, you said I couldn't go, so I'm wondering if I could go down to Beverly Hills with Demi Anderson and her mom."

He thought for a moment, recalling his conversation with Deana. "Maybe there's another option."

She frowned. "C'mon, you know Mrs. Anderson."

"I'm talking about Mexico."

She raised her brows.

"I'm not comfortable with you going there with people I don't know well, but if *I* were to take you …"

Her eyes widened. "You'd take me to Mexico?"

"It's not an easy week to take off from work—first quarter earnings reports need to be finalized—but I'll make it work."

Lucy squealed and nearly knocked over her smoothie bowl in her hurry to embrace him. He nearly dropped his cup of tea as she threw her arms around him.

She pulled back. "Wait, where in Mexico?

"Where is your guy Wilson going to be?"

"Ixtapa, I think."

"Then we'll go to Ixtapa. It'll give me a chance to get to know Wilson better."

She tightened her embrace. He smiled to himself. At least he could make one woman happy.

"Wilson will be so excited to meet you—and nervous, probably, given all that I've told him."

"You told him I'm a tyrant."

"Yeah, that."

"I reserve the right to resume my tyranny at any moment."

"Okay, okay," she said as she returned to her seat. Happy, Lucy fell upon her breakfast with improved appetite. "How's Bella?"

"Doing better, so I've heard."

"You're not … interested in her?"

He raised his brows at her derisive tone. "No, why?"

Lucille righted her bowl. "She never struck me as your type."

Deana came instantly to mind. He pushed the vision of her away, but he humored Lucy. "And what do you think is 'my type?'"

"One that makes you happy."

"Ah, it's that simple."

"I don't know exactly, but someone with less drama than Bella. Someone who knows how to appreciate you and who isn't so self-centered."

Someone like Deana, he thought to himself. He should try calling her again, but what if she refused to pick up again?

He had a better idea.

CHAPTER 18

"**M**ay I?" Deana smiled at the blonde-haired man as he held the door open for her. This was the second night in a week that he'd spoken to her, and she suspected he was flirting. From what she'd been told, he was a decent guy who worked as a paralegal at a law firm. She liked his manners and his friendly face, though she would've preferred a taller man. But she was ready to move on from Halsten Rockwell, though the first week back from the Chateau Follet had been hard. She craved his company; she craved his touch. Bereft of his attentions, she felt tense and irritable. No amount of self-pleasure, of which there were many in the loneliness of night, satisfied her longing.

She had seen his number pop up on her cell, but his voice message was just about checking in to make sure she made it back to the city okay. She probably could've called him back, but she didn't want to reopen a chapter she had thought finished.

Her luck had improved since finding the new card room outside the city in Oakland. Though the balance of what she'd received from Rockwell was sufficient to sustain the family for some time, she wanted a distraction, to keep her from dwelling on him. She couldn't bring herself to return to her old grounds for fear that she might encounter Rockwell. So, Gabby had recommended her to a friend, who invited Deana to play in his club, to make the games more challenging for the other patrons. The new club was much smaller and its appearance more modest, but after two weeks, she'd become acclimated to her new environment.

Deana stepped out into the summer night and turned to him. "Thank you. It's Patrick, right?"

"And you're Deana? I heard you're one of the best at poker."

"I'm a little more than competent but hardly the best."

"You're modest, Deana."

A light wind blew at them as they regarded each other in a moment of quiet.

Then a voice called from inside the club, "Pat! Your turn!"

"Would you like to play with me sometime?" Patrick said hastily.

"I could."

"Tomorrow night?"

"Pat Billings!" the voice called again.

She smiled. "Tomorrow night."

He returned her smile, his happiness obvious, and waved before turning back inside. She pulled out her wallet to check the balance on her train ticket back to the city was enough. A sudden gust of wind blew the ticket from her hand. She turned around, but someone had retrieved it from the ground.

"Still tempting danger, Deana?"

She froze as she drank in the sight of Rockwell. He held the ticket for her. Her heart throbbed painfully in her. She hadn't prepared herself for such a meeting.

"I once said that you had sense and wisdom," Rockwell continued. "But walking alone at night through sketchy neighborhoods like this isn't smart. Didn't I advise you against it?"

Her rancor allowed her to find her wits, and she took the ticket from him.

"Halsten Rockwell," she greeted, noting that he looked every bit as handsome, even in the dark, as when she'd last seen him. Of course, only two weeks, not two months or two years, had passed. How coincidental that their paths should've crossed in this neighborhood and on this street of all places.

"I'll take you back to the city."

She knew it was no use to protest and followed him to where his car waited. After assisting her into the vehicle, he seated himself and signaled to the driver. They sat in awkward silence as the car pulled out.

"How'd you find me?" she asked, wondering if Gabby had told him even though she had told her friend not to.

"I have my ways. How are your mother and aunt?" he asked, reminding her of a similar conversation that had eventually led them to the Chateau Follet.

"My mother has recovered well. It helps to know that you're not going to have be thrown out of your home. The doctor said she should be back to health if she takes her blood pressure medication and watches her stress levels," she replied. "How's your sister?"

"Lucy's happy. She's going to Mexico."

Deana looked at him with surprise. "You're letting her go? With the guy she's interested in?"

"Not exactly. She's going with me. If her guy happens to be there and they want to spend some time together, I don't mind—as long as I know where, when and what."

"She okay with that?"

"It's better than not going to Mexico at all, right?"

"I'm glad you found a compromise."

"Well, I was set on her not going to Mexico, but you got me to think less black and white about it."

She returned a smile. They fell once more into silence. Though it was dark and she'd be out of his presence soon enough, she wished she'd taken more care with her appearance. The sleeves of her top were a bit frayed at the edges, and she had a hole hidden at the pit of one arm. Rockwell, in contrast, was sharply dressed in a two-piece suit, tie and perfectly starched shirt.

She searched her mind for other topics to pass the time. She didn't want to ask about Bella even though she was curious if he and Bella were together. Asking about the Chateau or Madame Follet might also lead the conversation into unwanted territory.

"Why the new club?" he asked abruptly.

She shifted uncomfortably to delay answering.

"I was having a run of bad luck at Gabby's," she said carefully. "I thought a change of scenery …"

He studied her and seemed dubious. She avoided his gaze and glanced at the stately buildings lining the street.

"We've taken a wrong turn," she said and realized that they were in the Marina, where he lived.

"I thought we'd have a nightcap—a nonalcoholic one, like tea —at my place."

This wasn't good. She didn't want to have tea at his house. In her mind, she'd bid him goodbye for the last time.

"I have other plans," she objected.

The car felt small, and she occasionally bumped against his arm.

He raised his brows. "At midnight."

"Other intentions," she rephrased.

"At midnight."

She screamed inside her head. The man could not be more irritating!

"I'm kind of offended that you think I don't have anything better to do than to jump at your attention," she asserted.

The car stopped in front of his house. Stubbornly, she remained seated. "You told me you'd see me home."

"And I will, after our nightcap." He offered his hand.

"Why not now?"

"Because we're having tea."

She clenched her teeth. "I'd prefer to go home now."

"You know you never did show me your artwork."

"You weren't really that interested in my art, were you?"

"Ouch."

"That's okay. I didn't go to Chateau Follet to show off my paintings anyway."

"Will you show them to me now?"

"It's late. I'm kind of tired. Maybe another time," she lied.

"Okay. We'll just do the tea then."

She sighed in exasperation. "I'm—"

"Look, have tea this one time, then you don't have to worry about seeing me ever again."

She pressed her lips together. She was curious why he wanted to have her over, and she did want to spend time with Rockwell, even if it caused her pain. Rockwell took her hand and helped her out of the car. She noted the encompassing warmth of his grasp. The man had remarkable hands.

Stop it already, she told herself. She pulled at her hand, but he held it a few beats longer than necessary.

If he expects a willing and cheerful guest, he's wrong, Deana told herself. She intended to be done with tea as quickly as possible.

Midnight tea. Ha!

She followed him inside and into the room where she'd sat over a year ago. Nothing about the room had changed. She remembered the bronze oil lamp above the fireplace and the tapestry of Rati, wearing a golden headdress, arms stretched with a bow and arrow, astride a many-hued parrot. She flushed at the significance of the Indian goddess of love and physical pleasure.

"Have a seat, Deana," he indicated.

She sat at stiff attention on the sofa without removing her sweater or releasing her bag.

"You often keep your staff up at such late hours?" she asked when a man set down a tray on the table between them.

Seating himself across from her, he smiled at her attempt to censure his treatment of his employees.

She helped herself to the tea and cookies, as it was useful to avoid conversing with him. Why had he brought her to his place for tea? Was he bored and in need of a companion? Did he have an ... urge ... when he saw her coming out of the club and no one else to seek in the middle of the night? She found herself wanting an answer to her questions. She looked over at him to find him appraising her.

"How's Bella?" she asked the question she had not wanted to ask.

"She's currently in Scotland with relatives."

Ah. That was why he was in need of company. She sipped her tea and waited for him to speak, but he only continued his observation of her.

"This is a nice tea," she said.

"It is a chai blend of cardamom, nutmeg and black tea from the Himalayas. Try it with milk."

He picked up the small vessel. She held out her cup and saucer. He held her saucer still, his hand upon hers in the process. Her heart palpitated an uneven rhythm.

"Yum," she acknowledged, then proceeded to finish the beverage quickly to hasten the end of the tea.

"More?"

"No, thank you."

They sat staring at each another until impatience and insecurity forced her to her feet. She walked around the room, pretending to analyze the décor, conscious of his gaze on her.

"How long do you intend to keep me here?" she asked, feeling more at ease now that she could more easily avoid looking into his eyes.

"I'm holding you hostage?"

"Yes."

"You have a problem with my company?"

She frowned. It was an unfair question. "I'm just puzzled as to why you're interested in mine."

"Do you really?"

"I thought we finished our arrangement."

"Would you care for another?"

She looked at him sharply, then returned to looking at the walls, stopping before the tapestry of Rati. She felt angry. She'd put him out of her life, had met another man with whom she might have a chance, and he had the gall to reappear and ask her for *another arrangement?*

"Look," she said, fueling her courage through anger, "I'm not always at your beck and call, available whenever you want. I'm not your booty call."

Feeling his presence, she whirled around. In the next instant, his mouth was over hers. She struggled, but his arm was around her, crushing her to him without give. She pushed against his hard body. He circled his hands around both her wrists and pinned them above her head as he pushed her up against the wall. His mouth assaulted hers with frightful force and suffocating breadth. She panicked, not because he might try to impose his will on her. She would never think him capable of such an offense—no, she panicked because her body was responding to him.

"What is the safeword?" he growled as he devoured her neck and shoved his hips into her.

Holding her wrists in one hand, he untied her scarf and tossed it to the floor. She closed her eyes against the onslaught, trying to pick up the fragments of her anger as her traitorous body succumbed to the longing she had kept at bay.

"Hey!" she said, to herself as much as him.

"Safeword, Deana."

His hand went to her sweater, tearing it open. The buttons clattered to the floor. She twisted against his grip.

"You've got some nerve—"

"What is the safeword?" he demanded.

She stared into his molten eyes. *Good God*, he wanted her. The realization heated her loins and caused her pussy to ache.

But he'll be back to Bella tomorrow.

"Haven't you heard a word?" she cried.

He managed to shove his hand down her dress to cup a breast. She groaned despite herself.

Abruptly, he tore her from the wall and toward a door that she recognized all too well despite her single acquaintance with it.

"I think you'll want your safeword," he said as he pulled her inside.

With chains, shackles, crops, and floggers, the room could've fit easily into the East Wing of Chateau Follet. She saw a wooden chair, and treacherous memories of how he had bent her over the back of it made her hot with desire. Would he do the same tonight or did he have other plans?

"Well?" he prompted.

She said nothing, her mind searching for how she was to extract herself from the situation.

He was standing behind her, cupping her neck, tilting her chin up, his mouth beside her ear.

"Do not keep me waiting much longer, Deana."

CHAPTER 19

Her legs threatened to liquefy. She'd always found his voice sensual, the sound of her name on his lips wickedly enticing.

"Rati," she whispered.

How was it she couldn't refrain from submitting to Halsten Rockwell?

He turned her head so that he could access her lips. His mouth was more controlled this time, probing and commanding. With his lips and tongue, he enticed hers into a sensual dance. Desire pooled low and hot in her abdomen. He released her head. His mouth trailed across her jaw, down her neck, and to the edge of her décolletage. His hands grasped her open sweater and pulled it down past her shoulders, pinioning her arms. As his mouth continued to caress her about the neck, he pulled her top over her head and onto her arms. He went for her bra next.

"I like the front close," he noted with approval.

With her back still pinned to his chest, he undid the clasp. He pulled the straps down her arms as well. She now had three layers of garments—her sweater, top, and bra—locking her arms uncomfortably to her body. He palmed both breasts and rubbed her nipples. They pressed against his hand. He rolled and tugged at the points of flesh between his thumbs and forefingers. She writhed against him. As she became more and more aroused, his touch became harder. The attention was devastating. She didn't know whether to bend away or arch her back further into him. The ache in her cunt throbbed angrily.

Taking her by a nipple, he pulled her over to a chair, the very chair he had bent her over the last time she was here. This time he sat in it, pulled her skirt to her thighs, and positioned her over his lap. He parted his legs, forcing hers open. With her arms pinioned, she felt unbalanced and had to concentrate to stay on top of him. Reaching under her skirt, he found the moisture between her thighs.

"This pleases me, Deana," he said, swirling his fingers in her wetness.

She groaned. Her body began perspiring. An agonizing tension had built within her, and only he could release it.

"In due time," he murmured as if reading her mind. He began to rub and torment her clit, his gaze intent on her reactions.

He took a breast in his mouth. She nearly toppled from his lap as he sucked her tit while toying with her other highly sensitive nub. He put a hand to her hip to hold her steady. Moaning, she writhed at the pleasurable assault. She'd been right to submit to him, her body signaled. She'd already done so in the past. One more night wouldn't matter and could only bring such delights as she was unlikely to ever experience again.

His mouth sucked, his hand fondled with increasing vigor. The pressure within her was just about to reach boiling point when he released her. As if she'd been hit with a wall of fresh air, she inhaled at the sudden deprivation. He put her back on her feet.

"Take off your clothes," he instructed as he began to loosen his tie.

Eager to return to her earlier progress, she struggled to pull her arms free. It was no easy task for the garments on top had secured the ones beneath. Rockwell, also disrobing, had a much easier time as he cast his tie onto the back of the chair and began to unbutton his shirt. As she struggled with her attire, she found herself mesmerized by the calm with which he undressed, revealing his broad and chiseled chest, arms, and torso. She drank in his splendor.

"Don't delay, Deana," he said as he retrieved a crop.

Doubling her efforts, she wiggled and jumped, her unrestrained breasts bouncing with the exertion, but the tight sleeves of the sweater were caught. The crop fell against her backside, its sting blunted by her clothing. Nonetheless she yelped. Straining one hand, she reached for the cuff of her sweater. The crop fell against the side of a breast. With a hasty yank, she pulled the sleeve and the sweater slipped from under the sleeve of the top and the strap of the bra. He struck her thigh. Quickly, she shimmied her arms out of the garments and pushed them to the floor. Her shoees and panties followed.

He pulled her arms together behind her back until her elbows touched and tied her arms in place with her bra. The position forced her breasts forward. He ran a finger along the tops and bottoms of her breasts. He tapped the crop against one orb.

"I think I'll leave these free for tonight."

She barely heard his words, though it almost sounded as if this was not to be their only night together. She would have to make clear later that she had no wish to see him ever again, but for now, she only wanted him to continue his sublime agony.

The crop bit at a nipple. She cried out. He massaged the affected breast and kissed the smarting nipple. He flicked at it repeatedly with his tongue, and she groaned as the fire in her belly stirred. She watched him walk over to a chest of drawers. After opening and shutting a drawer, he returned to her holding a pair of small clamps joined together by a thin chain.

"Devon should have started with these," he said.

She gritted her teeth at the sharp pinching pain on her nipples. The clamps were not nearly as bad as what had been used at Chateau Follet. But the relativity didn't matter. The hellish things on her now hurt plenty. Her toes curled.

"Breathe."

She focused on her breath and found her tolerance for the pain.

"Well done."

He tugged at the chain. The clamps pulled at her nipples. Tears pressed the backs of her eyes. He brushed his lips against her temple.

"You are a sight to behold."

His words encouraged and enflamed her. She wanted to withstand everything he would do to show him how capable and strong she was. She wanted him to reward her.

He led her back to the chair and sat down. He had her stand astride him. To her delight, he undid his pants and pulled out his very solid cock. She hoped he'd let her take possession of the erection soon. He rubbed himself slowly so that his cock lengthened to its limits. He pointed it between her thighs.

"Bend your legs."

Yes!

She lowered herself.

"Stop," he commanded just as the tip grazed her pussy.

She looked at him curiously.

"Fall and pay the price," he said.

No.

He rubbed the bulbous head along her slit. It felt wonderful, but she wanted his cock to touch the deepest part of her. He pressed his cock at her clit, and she closed her eyes to further relish the pleasure. Back and forth he worked his cock. Coated in her wetness, it slid easily along her. Beautiful, delicious sensations fanned from her cunt. But squatting over his cock was an awkward exertion, and her legs soon began to tremble. Surely, he would let her take him at any moment?

She grunted as beads of sweat formed along her brow. "Sir—"

The labor required to stay in position distracted from her ascent toward climax.

He increased the rubbing, pushing it at her perineum. She quivered in delight. But her legs threatened to buckle beneath her. If only she could come before …

Her legs gave way. She sank onto his lap, sheathing his cock in her pussy. The feel of him inside of her was nothing short of wonderful. For a second, she didn't care that she hadn't succeeded in keeping the position he wanted. She looked at him through lowered lashes, but instead of a frown, she saw his eyes gleaming.

"Suit yourself, Deana."

It was hardly a choice! she wanted to say. Her muscles simply could not persevere. They had no practice in crouching for lengths of time.

He twisted a finger in the chain between her nipple clamps. They pulled at her, renewing the pain there. At least he had allowed his cock to remain in place.

"Make yourself come."

She blinked. Well, she wasn't about to remind him that he had mentioned a 'price to pay' earlier. Taking his offer, she worked her hips, trying to push his cock as deep inside her as she could. He continued to twist the chain. His other hand found her clit, slick and engorged. The triple stimulation, his cock inside her, his thumb at her clitoris, the clamps pulling at her, combined to send her over the edge. He snapped the clamps off her nipples just as she imploded with a bloodcurdling scream. She would have convulsed right off his lap if he hadn't caught her hip. Shuddering violently, she fell against him, her hot and sweaty body against his.

She murmured an oath, then realized she'd spoken it aloud.

Recovering from her raptures, she found him stroking her back tenderly. She stirred slightly and felt he was still hard inside of her. Oh dear, that meant she wasn't finished.

"Pleased?"

The strange inquiry made her look at him. He was gazing at her as if searching her face for something.

"A little," she teased.

"Good. On your knees."

She stood up, glad to stretch her legs, then knelt on the cold, hard ground. He stood, his cock at her face. She opened her mouth willingly, wanting to give him the same pleasure he'd provided her. He slid his cock inside of her. She tasted her own wetness on him, unsure of how she regarded her own flavor. With her arms still bound behind her, she couldn't exert herself as well on his shaft, so he fisted a hand in her hair and guided her mouth. She tried to take him down her throat as much as possible and managed to suppress most of her gagging reflexes.

His eyes closed, and he grunted his enjoyment.

"Suck. Harder."

She obliged until her cheeks hurt. He tensed further, and she sensed his end was near. He bucked his hips at her, and with a roar, he shoved himself deep into her. Warm, tangy liquid filled her mouth. She swallowed to prevent from choking as he pumped his seed into her. His legs shook, and his fingers curled in her hair. Pleased that she could cause his surrender, she licked her lips after he'd pulled himself from her. He knelt down before her and kissed her. Reaching around her, he untied her bra. Relief rushed through her sore arms.

"And now, the price, Deana."

She cursed herself. The man hadn't forgotten. It was late, and she was tired. But her pride wouldn't allow her to ask for leniency.

After buttoning his trousers, he lifted her and placed her among the numerous plush pillows underneath a blood red canopy with golden tassels and orange curtains. He lay beside her and fitted his hand between her thighs. His languid strokes felt pleasant, but she wondered if she had the wherewithal to go another round.

"Have you thought of Chateau Follet since your departure?" he asked.

Many, many times.

"A few times," she replied.

"You have a favorite memory?"

She thought of all the times she'd been with him. How could she pick a favorite among them? For days afterward, she'd relived each one twice over.

"They were all an experience," she said. "I guess the night with Bella and Devon was memorable."

"In what way?"

His fingers had an intoxicating effect, putting her at ease while strumming a luscious tension.

"It felt as if I were undergoing two simultaneous sources of titillations, mine and theirs. I'd never witnessed another couple before. It was provocative. What Devon did ..."

She felt him stiffen. He rose. No doubt the mention of his rival didn't sit well with him. She chastised her carelessness.

Rockwell returned with a small box and wide iron bar with two shackles on either end of it. She sat up at attention and watched as he locked her ankles into the outer shackles. The bar prevented her legs from closing. He pushed her onto her back and locked her wrists into the two inner shackles.

Oh my God. Her cunt was exposed completely.

"Tell me more," he said as he wound the strange little box.

Fixated on the strange instrument he held, her mind drew a blank.

"Does Devon turn you on?"

"*Hmmmm?*"

"Does he excite you?"

"What's that you've got?"

"A Magic Wand. You've never seen or had one of these before?"

"No."

He sat down beside her and placed it at her pussy. She squealed as the wand vibrated against her. He allowed her a breath before replacing it on her. She wanted to snap her legs shut but couldn't. The sensation was jarring, and yet ...

"Oh ... oh!" she cried.

The sensations improved. Yes, much improved. It was an amazing device.

"Did you wonder what it might have felt like if you had been in Bella's place?"

Why was he asking her such a question?

"Did you?"

He pressed the wand harder on her. She shook her head.

"The truth."

She had thanked her stars she had been with Rockwell that evening, but she had also wondered if she could have endured what Bella had.

"I suppose," she murmured, desire blossoming once more.

"He wanted you."

Pleasure rippled through her from the wand.

"Did you want him?" Rockwell asked.

"Devon?" She let his question sink in. What was the purpose of this question? She wasn't interested in talking. She was interested in coming.

"Did you?"

"Did I?"

"Want Devon," he growled.

"No!"

The vibrations slowed. She prayed he'd use it again. Instead, he rose and placed the wand on the chair. She groaned in frustration.

"Rest. I'll be back."

She glared at him as he took a robe off the back of the door and slipped it on. He was leaving her? For how long?

"Please, don't be long," she said. "You said you would take me home."

He said nothing and closed the door behind him.

CHAPTER 20

Deana tried the shackles but found them secure. She growled in frustration. She was lying on her back with her arms and legs spread in the air. She glanced at the wand on the chair. Could she reach it? No, she'd have to crawl to it, but with her arms locked with her legs, there was no possibility she could maneuver herself there. She tried the shackles once more but without success. Her body had been poised to come again. Instead he'd left her in aggravation. Was this her punishment? She reached a hand toward her pussy to see if she could stroke herself, but her hands were locked too far away. Maybe if she found a way to rub herself on something? But she was surrounded only by soft pillows.

"*Aaargh,*" she muttered.

"Angry?"

He'd returned and stood in the doorway. He held a box, which he placed on top of the chest of drawers.

"I'm damned perfect," she replied.

He clucked his tongue as he approached. Sitting down beside her, he ran a finger along the length of her womanhood. She shivered.

"Need anything, Deana?" he teased, circling her clit.

She moaned. *I'm in need of you.*

"Do you want me to beg for it, sir?" she asked more flippantly than she intended.

His eyes steeled. "Would you?"

"If you want," she replied more sincerely. She glanced at the wand. Yes, she'd beg for those beautiful vibrations. Her gaze traveled to his crotch. Or better yet …

He dipped a finger into her cunt. She closed her eyes. Yes, she wanted him inside.

"Please, sir," she began.

"Please, what?"

She stared him in the eyes. "Please fuck me."

His gaze aflame, he withdrew. Slowly—much too slowly—he took off the rest of his clothes. His cock stood at proud attention. Kneeling against her bottom, he rubbed his shaft along her. He jerked himself against her clit, her pussy, her perineum until she was near to orgasm. Retreating, he spanked the expanse of flesh before him from the underside of her thighs to her buttocks and even across her hot, wet folds. She yelped at the slaps, but they fueled her lust. Her body knew no shame before this man.

"Fuck me," she implored.

"We didn't get our final night at Chateau Follet," he said, halting.

She strained for his hand to fondle her or smack her again. "Yes."

"A pity."

"*Yes.*"

"Is there anything you wish we could have done?"

"That you could have fucked me senseless."

He frowned. She thought he would have been happy with that answer. But in the next instant he was on her, his cock plunging deep into her. She cried out at the depth of his penetration. Her knees crushed the pillows beside her as he slammed his cock into her. She welcomed every ounce of force. Her body, tormented with lust, in need of the strongest relief, wanted the pounding, wanted him, wanted to drive out all possibility that there would remain some small grain of unsatisfied desire for him to taunt later.

They reached the pinnacle simultaneously, her cries mixed with his anguished grunts as their bodies bucked and shuddered against each other. Her pussy felt awash in warmth, throbbing, grasping. He trembled on top of her, pushed his hips at her a final time, and collapsed against her. They took in large, heaving breaths, their perspiration mingling, as they lay joined together.

Gradually, the thundering of her heart receded and she became aware of his weight on her, pushing on the iron bar. He lifted himself off. He unlocked the shackles, kissed her ankles, and fell back once more beside her. He pulled her wrists to him and kissed the soreness there.

"Sorry if I was too rough," he said. "When you talk like that, it's like I turn into a demon. I just want to possess you to the hilt."

She sighed inside. She wished he could and would possess her in all ways. A part of her wanted to cry. Though she'd done her best to downplay her emotions for the past three months, she'd missed Rockwell greatly. And now she'd have to start again with her efforts to forget him. She shouldn't have come here tonight. She should've resisted his offer to take her home. She should've told him that she wished never to set eyes on him ever again.

"I'm not so fragile as you think," she replied, pulling her wrists away from him.

Her movement seemed to displease him. With his hair damp from perspiration, clinging in parts to his face, he looked provocative all naked and mussed. She turned from him, worried that the sentimental feelings stirring inside her might lead to tears.

"Who were you talking to at the club?" he asked.

"What?"

"The short blonde. As you were leaving."

"Pat Billings?"

"You guys close?"

"That's none of your business."

Irked, she sat up and intended to rise and retrieve her clothes, but he caught her arm.

"Why did you change clubs?"

She looked at him sharply. "You asked that already."

"I want the truth."

She wanted to scream. The glow of their lovemaking, if it could be called that, had dissipated, replaced by a mixture of anger, sadness, and even self-pity. She'd brought this on herself, true, but Fate had been most cruel to set before her a man to love but not have.

"You're trying to avoid me," he answered for her.

"So? I just didn't want to be reminded about the past. I'm not exactly proud that I had to resort to what I did."

She couldn't look him in the eye. This time when she made a move to rise, he didn't stop her. She would be quite sore tomorrow, in many parts of her body.

"What happens when the money runs out?"

Aloud, she said, "I'll find a way."

He watched her dress from where he was, still lying on the pillows.

"Deana, if you ever need help, don't hesitate to ask me."

"Don't worry about me. I'm quite resourceful."

"Yes, you are."

She finished with her top and skirt and reached for her sweater. The sooner she escaped his presence, the better for her.

"I have a proposition for you." *Damnation,* she groaned, *not another one.* He rose and went to the chest of drawers. On it was a large velvet box. He brought it over to her. "Humor me," he said as he opened the familiar container.

She stared at the exquisite jewelry she'd worn at Chateau

171

Follet. She hesitated. Hadn't she just determined that she had to leave as quickly as possible? But the ornaments called to her. He lifted the necklace and placed it around her neck, then the head-piece, earrings, and bracelet. She fingered the intricate web of the necklace.

He stepped back for a better view. "They belong with you."

"I said once before, gifts are unnecessary."

"You haven't heard my proposition yet."

Did he mean to offer her the jewels if she spent another night with him? If she returned to Chateau Follet with him? Was he not with Bella?

"I think Bella would enjoy these equally," she said.

His expression twisted oddly, and she admitted that her state-ment sounded rather stupid.

"Deana, if you interrupt me again, I'll whip your ass so hard it'll be a week before you can sit down."

She blinked. Damn, he meant it. Reluctantly, she remained silent. But she knew her answer already. Whatever he offered, she had to refuse.

"I want you to take the jewels, Deana, if you're not interested in seeing me anymore."

"I'm not taking the jewels—wait, what?"

Astonished, she watched him go down upon a knee.

"Deana Herwood, would you honor me by becoming my sub?"

Was he joking? Had she heard him correctly?

"What does that mean exactly?" she ventured.

"It means you're mine."

"But what about Bella?" she asked, still confused.

Rockwell looked annoyed. "What about Bella?"

"Aren't you guys …?"

"No. We dated once, but I would never do it again. She was a family friend in need of help. You're the one I want. Do you know how many hours I've spent in the last week searching for you? I must've gone to every gaming club in the city—twice. I made inquiries everywhere."

She felt a little sheepish. He had been searching for her? Had she totally misconstrued the situation with Bella?

"I thought," he continued, "if I could show you, remind you, of the fun we had, you'd reconsider wanting to be with me. I've thought of nothing else but you since leaving Chateau Follet. I have to have you. I can't just hope that you'll lose at cards every time I want to be with you."

Moved by his imploring gaze and the glow from her heart, she sank to her knees before him, still hardly able to believe what she heard.

"You want me to be your sub?" she asked.

"Well, more than just my sub. I want you in every way possible. I can't stand the thought of you with another man. And I can't stand the thought of never seeing you again."

He took both her hands and brought them to his lips, his eyes shining with anticipation. As the full realization of what he asked, of his feelings for her, sank in, she could barely contain her euphoria. She choked on the intensity of emotions.

"So I keep the jewelry only if I turn you down?" she inquired, her voice unsteady. "They are really pretty ..."

He frowned.

"But of course I'd rather have you."

He grasped her face in both his hands and smothered her mouth with his. She submitted willingly, deliciously, to the kiss and returned it with her own fervor. She wanted to laugh. She wanted to cry. But most of all she wanted to show him the depths of her feelings for him.

"Deana," he murmured against her lips. "My Deana."

She'd be forever grateful that she'd lost that fateful hand at cards to Halsten Rockwell. She wrapped her arms possessively around him, feeling the full smile of Lady Luck on her.

I hope you enjoyed this romance. Reviews are much appreciated. And for more sizzling erotic romance, read on for the first part of BOUND TO HIM.

EXCERPT OF BOUND TO HIM

CHAPTER 1

C hen He Lee held back a grimace as he walked into the hospital room and beheld Peter, his head wrapped in bandages, his face purple and swollen. Peter had put on a significant amount of weight since Chen had last seen him several years ago, and Chen would not have been surprised if the small hospital bed beneath Peter collapsed at any second. Beside the bed, the heart-rate monitor beeped slowly but steadily.

I should have done better to stay in touch, Chen thought with regret.

Peter Wong had been Chen's best friend through seven years of boarding school in London, but after high school, Chen had gone off to Oxford and then the London Business School, while Peter had returned home to Shanghai, presumably to take over the family's failing import-export business.

After getting his MBA, Chen had gone straight into his own family's multibillion-dollar business. The long hours and international travel had made it hard to stay in touch with old friends. He might not have even known that Peter had been shot if not for a former classmate who had come across a news post about it on WeChat.

"A vision from my past," Peter greeted in a weak voice.

Chen approached and looked Peter over. He had a dozen questions but did not want to task his friend's fragile state. Keeping his tone light, he said, "You look like shit."

Peter grunted. "Says the pretty boy."

Chen smiled, but on the inside, he seethed. He was going to find the bastard or bastards who did this.

Peter started coughing, and Chen reached for the water pitcher beside the bed. Peter lifted his hand, the one that didn't have IV's taped to it.

"I need...a favor," he said.

Chen leaned in.

"Take care of my..." He stopped to gasp for breath.

Chen pulled back. "You should rest. You can tell me about it later."

"No. My swan—take care..." His eyes widened as he drew in another difficult breath. "Promise me."

"I promise," Chen replied, not wanting his friend to agitate himself.

"There's a...in kitchen..."

Peter grimaced. At that moment, a nurse entered and addressed Chen. "If you please, Mr. Lee, the patient needs to rest. The police were in here asking questions earlier. You can come back tomorrow."

"I'd like to come back later today," Chen replied.

"I'm afraid there are no more visiting hours for today."

Not satisfied with her response, he merely looked at her till, blushing beneath his stare, she relented.

"If your visit is a short one," she said.

Chen took his leave, walking by the station where three nurses were obviously conversing about him, but he was accustomed to the attention he received.

After departing the hospital, he decided to stop by the local police to see what they knew, which was disappointingly little. In fact, shortly into the conversation, Chen felt as if the police considered *him* a suspect.

"We have indications that Peter was involved with the *Jing San*," one of the police officers explained. "That triad is comprised of a lot of Lees, isn't it?"

"That's the other side of the family," Chen replied. "Not my side."

The *Jing San* represented the lesser-known criminal members of the Lee family. The rest of the Lee family had built a legitimate fortune worth over ten billion US dollars through real estate developments, venture capital funding, tech investments and old-fashioned property ownership.

Done with the police, Chen called his primary executive assistant to say that he would be out of the office for several days. After wrapping up a few business calls and one to a private investigator in case the police couldn't or wouldn't do their job, Chen returned to the hospital.

But Peter's room was empty.

Chen found a nurse and inquired into Peter.

"Mr. Wong experienced a sudden drop in blood pressure. He was taken down to the emergency room an hour ago," she replied, then looked down, avoiding his gaze. "I'm afraid he didn't make it."

With a frown, Chen surveyed the studio apartment strewn with dirty laundry, Japanese pornography, and wastebaskets overfilled with takeout boxes and disposable chopsticks. This was how Peter had lived before he was killed?

Standing beside Chen, the landlord grimaced at the sight. "Are you certain you want to enter? You might dirty your expensive clothes and shoes."

The older man looked over Chen's cashmere sweater and the

designer loafers Chen had bought on his last trip through Italy. The shoes alone probably cost more than what Peter paid in rent the whole year.

Chen stepped over several empty beer bottles and made his way to the kitchen table. He moved aside a pack of cigarettes, a stack of bills, and a magazine of hentai. Beneath it lay a cellphone.

Surprised that the police hadn't taken it, Chen pocketed the device. He'd have his favorite hacker in Singapore take a crack at it.

He walked over to the refrigerator, which was covered in pictures of women, all naked except for one, which Chen plucked off the door and examined. A young woman with long brown hair smiled shyly from behind a pair of large, dark sunglasses. She might have been a model except that she didn't look particularly comfortable in the skimpy clothes she was wearing.

He replaced the photo and looked over the kitchen. He wasn't entirely sure what he was looking for.

It sounded like Peter had said "swan," but maybe Chen had misheard. In Chinese, a slight change in intonation led to the pronunciation of an entirely different word. Chen went through the other possibilities, but none of them made sense either.

"If you want, I can pack up all his belongings for you," the landlord said. "I charge only two hundred yuan."

"Not yet," Chen replied as he opened cabinet doors in the kitchen to find mostly empty shelves except for a few packets of instant noodles and a dead mouse. He looked out the small kitchen window—straight into the kitchen window of the next apartment building.

A middle-aged woman with disheveled hair glared back at him. "What are you looking at?"

She threw the contents of her mug into the sink. The thin window panes failed to muffle her words as she muttered, "Nosy dog fart."

Chen turned back around and surveyed the kitchen once more. Peter must have misspoken. Maybe the bullet to his head had messed with his brain's wiring.

"Leave me the key," Chen told the landlord.

The man shook his head. "Your friend is two months past due on the rent. I should have rented this place to someone else a long time ago. I'll have to pay a lot of money to have this place cleaned before I can lease it again."

Chen didn't bother replying that he doubted there would be a lot of takers for the dump even after it was cleaned. Instead, he took out his wallet, pulled out several hundreds and handed them to the landlord. "This should take care of all your concerns."

The landlord's eyes widened as he went through the bills. He bobbed his head up and down. "Yes, yes. You are a good friend of Mr. Wong. Very good friend."

After handing Chen the key, the landlord left in obvious good spirits.

Setting his hands on his hips, Chen surveyed the apartment once more. Maybe Peter thought the "swan" was in the kitchen and had forgotten he'd moved it?

Fuck.

If only he had stayed a little longer by Peter's side. If only he had kept in touch, he could have helped Peter out, given him money or a job, helped him sort out his family's business. Instead, he had allowed his own obligations and interests take precedence. What a shit friend he was. In grammar school, when Chen was a scrawny boy the bullies liked to pick on, Peter had been his protector. When Chen and Peter had gotten back at the bullies by mixing piss with soda and passing it off as Mountain Dew, it was Peter who had volunteered to take responsibility when the headmaster found out. Peter deserved more than what he had gotten in life.

Fuck.

Chen wanted to drive his fist through the wall, but the mobile in his pocket buzzed. Taking out Peter's phone, Chen read the text:

Van will pick up at 10AM tomorrow. Only one piece of luggage allowed. Have 35,000 ¥ in cash ready.

Whoever had sent the text clearly didn't know that Peter was dead, but Chen couldn't help but suspect that it had something to do with Peter's murder. 35,000 ¥ was about five thousand US dollars and nothing to sneeze at. And given Peter's living conditions, it didn't seem he had that kind of money on hand.

Chen took out his own cellphone to call Sanjiv.

"I'll get on it, but it'll take time. It's not easy hacking into a Chinese telecomm giant," Sanjiv said. "I could do it faster if I have the SIM card."

"You'll have to manage without. I want to see all incoming calls and texts for now."

After hanging up, Chen weighed telling the police about the text, but the *Jing San* was known to have police on their payroll. Chen decided he would keep the text to himself for now. He would be ready for this 10AM pick up.

CHAPTER 2

"**A**re you nervous about marrying a man you never met?"

Alena Vetrov watched the blond, a young Russian woman not unlike herself, vie for space with half a dozen other women to examine her makeup for the tenth time before one of two mirrors in the room of a hotel in Blagoveshchensk, a city bordering China and located at the confluence of the Amur and Zeya rivers.

"Yes," Alena replied to Natasha, thinking perhaps she should check her makeup as well, though the only cosmetic she had applied was lip-gloss because that was all she could afford. She did not reveal to the woman she had befriended on the twelve-hour drive to Blagoveshchensk that marrying a stranger was nothing new to her. At the ripe old age of twenty-four, she had been married three times already.

But this would be the fourth and last time, she assured herself as she fiddled with the simple cocktail dress she wore. She hadn't wanted to go through a sham marriage again just for the money, but there were no jobs to be had in her economically depressed hometown, and she had her mother, Olga, and Babushka to support.

There was still a chance for her to pull out, and she very much wanted to. Not only because she felt dishonest about marrying a man she intended to ditch right after the wedding, but because she had a strange sensation that something was going to go wrong this time. She wasn't superstitious, but four was considered an unlucky number in Chinese culture because the pronunciation of the number, sì, was similar to the pronunciation of the word for death, sǐ. Her third husband had refused to stay on the fourth floor of any building because of it.

"What does your guy look like?" asked Natasha after applying another coat of mascara.

"I don't know," Alena answered, then bit her bottom lip. She hadn't heard from Peter Wong—whom she had gotten to know through the matchmaking agency's online chat room—in over three days, which was unusual because Peter corresponded daily.

He had been interested in her early on, and his enthusiasm had only grown when she'd shared a photo of herself—Olga had insisted Alena pose for the photo in a cropped shirt and a pair of shorts one size too small.

Peter hadn't shared one of himself, explaining that he wanted a woman who didn't judge a man on appearance. To Alena, it didn't matter if he was old, short, fat, ugly or all of the above. All that mattered was that he had money, and most Chinese men who could afford the agency's fees did.

Peter's last message to her had expressed his excitement that they would finally be meeting in person, affirmed his love for her, and assured her that he would have her dowry of two million rubles, in cash, as she had requested. It was the largest sum she had ever sought.

She hadn't wanted to ask for that much, but after much prodding from Olga, she had lied to Peter, telling him that her mother had been diagnosed with cancer and would need extensive treatment. Peter had responded that he would happily support whatever she and her mother needed, and that she should never hesitate to ask how he might be able to help.

But maybe he had changed his mind? Or maybe he didn't have the money.

"Mine has a nice smile," said Natasha. "I only hope he's not too short."

"Mine has a receding hairline," remarked another woman, adjusting her strapless dress, "but he says he's the chief engineer at his company. He must make good money. He takes care of his parents and five younger siblings."

"That's all I want," sighed the oldest of the women, at thirty-one years of age, "a man who's dedicated to his family, who's responsible and wants children, who doesn't get drunk on vodka every other night."

A murmur of agreement swept through the throng of women. Alena felt their pain. Her own father had been known to drink far too often and died early of liver disease.

"I don't think Chinese men drink a lot of vodka, if at all."

"My husband, may he rot in peace, wasn't a drunkard," piped a raven-haired beauty. "He was just stupid. Got in a fight with another man twice his size because he had to prove his masculinity. He died from a single punch to the throat."

"Thank God China has more than enough men to compensate for the dearth here."

China's previous one-child policy had led to a gender imbalance, as many Chinese families favored boys over girls. The matchmaking agency that Alena had signed up with was just one of many that facilitated relationships between Russian women and Chinese men. The agency even provided Chinese language classes, and Alena felt she had an elementary-grade proficiency in Mandarin. She enjoyed languages and was nearly fluent in English. She had hoped to get a job teaching English, but that would require moving to a larger city.

"And leave me to take care of Babushka on my own?" Olga

had argued when they'd had this conversation before. "And what kind of job would pay you enough to cover our rent plus your own? You have no college degree, and your only work experience is waiting tables."

The two million rubles from Peter, plus the bonus she would receive from the matchmaking agency after they were married, would buy her enough time to hopefully find a situation that could satisfy her mother. All she had to do was marry Peter, whom she would meet as soon as the women were done primping and preening, collect her money and leave. The matchmaking agency claimed that half their matches ended in marriage, some within a day of the initial meeting.

Feeling nervous, Alena scooped up her tabby, George.

"You're not bringing the cat?" Olga had asked of the skinny feline. "What if your husband-to-be is allergic to the thing?"

"Well, I won't be with the groom for long, will I?" Alena had replied.

From where she'd sat by the window of the living room with several blankets covering her to keep warm, as the heater was kept low to save money, Babushka had coughed and waved a dismissive hand at Olga. "Let her have the cat. The Chinese consider cats to be lucky."

Olga had put her hands on her hips. "I thought the Chinese considered them *un*lucky and that is why there are no cats in their zodiac. Dogs, roosters, and monkeys. No cats."

"No cats? Are you certain? Then why are there so many of these?" Babushka had picked up her walking cane and pointed toward the three porcelain cats smiling from the windowsill. The figurines were gifts from Alena's first Chinese husband.

Ignoring her mother, Olga had returned her critical eye to Alena. "The cat makes you look sallow."

"Leave her be. She is beautiful enough—a little too thin, but at least her breasts are of a decent size."

Olga had pinched a tendril of light brown hair that had come loose from Alena's bun. "Maybe we should have dyed your hair blond."

For once, Alena had agreed with her mother's suggestion regarding her appearance. A different hair color would help conceal her identity. She worried that she would be recognized, perhaps by one of her own husbands, though she was careful to work with a different matchmaking agency each time.

An older woman from the agency entered the hotel room and clapped her hands. "Time to meet the men."

She corralled the women outside to the top of the stairs, which wound down to the hotel lobby.

"Remember: enter like a princess at a ball," the agency woman told them.

Alena looked over the sea of black hair that had congregated at the bottom of the stairs. The men varied in age, with some in their mid-20s and others in their mid-40s. All were dressed formally in suits except for one man, who stood several inches taller than most of the others. He was dressed more casually in a button-down shirt and slacks, but Alena found him the most impressive.

Natasha must have had the same sentiment, murmuring, "*O bozhe*, I wish mine looked like that one."

More built than the other men, he looked to be in his late 20s or early 30s. He had a wide brow, strong jawline, and large almond-shaped eyes. She wondered why a man as attractive as him would need to go through a matchmaking agency to find a wife.

Realizing the man was staring back at her, she quickly looked away. Her heartbeat quickened. There was something unnerving about the man. He didn't look as eager and excited as the other men. Rather, he looked serious…and intense.

She had left George back in the changing room but now wished she had the comfort of the furry bundle. At least that man was unlikely to be Peter, who had come across much more humorous and lighthearted in the chat room.

One by one, the women descended the stairs as their names were called. A man from the group would step up to greet them. After the first few women had been called, Alena glanced back at the imposing man, startled to find him still looking at her.

She flushed. Had he been staring at her the whole time? She was hardly the prettiest. Dubbing the man Solemn One, she decided she would not look at him again no matter how much her gaze was drawn in his direction.

When there were only three men left at the bottom of the stairs and three women at the top, Alena heard her name called.

One of the men, among the youngest in the group, held a bouquet of flowers. Alena hoped that was Peter. Or maybe the older man with sunspots would be less heartbroken when she married, then deserted him. Either one would be better than Solemn One, who continued to frown at her.

Why was he still looking at her?

Discombobulated, Alena nearly tripped on the first step and had to grab the rail to save herself from an embarrassing tumble down the stairs. Straightening, she put on a smile and managed to make her way down to the bottom, though the four-inch heels she was unaccustomed to wearing did not make the descent easy. She made eye contact with the young man with flowers. His smile broadened as he bobbed his head.

But the man who stepped forward was Solemn One.

CHAPTER 3

Chen noticed that her smile fell into a frown at beholding him.

It was her. The woman whose photo he had seen on Peter's refrigerator. Could this woman possibly be involved with Peter's death?

With an unassuming demeanor, she didn't come across as a criminal. But criminals came in all shapes and sizes. Beautiful ones, too. Like this one.

On the long drive over flat terrain to Heihe in Heilongjiang Province, before crossing the border to Blagoveshchensk, many of the other nine other men in the van talked of how beautiful Russian women were. They made generalizations that Russian women were less materialistic and better in bed.

It seemed unlikely that a matchmaking service would want Peter dead. They didn't even seem to know he had died.

"Peter Wong?" the driver had confirmed upon picking Chen up at Peter's apartment. "You have the thirty-five thousand?"

Chen had taken out his money clip and paid the man. Not wanting to come across as ostentatious, he had left his more expensive items behind. The driver had accepted Chen as Peter, or the man simply didn't care who was who as long as the money was there.

The matchmaking agency may or may not have anything to do with Peter's death, but following the money trail usually led to answers.

"*Ni hao,*" the woman, Alena, said in halfway decent Mandarin. She gave him a smile.

With Peter's death still on his mind and the possibility that this woman might be connected, Chen wasn't in the mood to be friendly, but he wasn't going to get anywhere by being frosty.

"*Privet,*" he returned in Russian.

Her countenance brightened, making her prettier. "*Otlichno.*"

But she continued to look at him with some misgiving. She spoke in accented English next. "It is nice to see you finally. I said correctly, yes?"

He returned a puzzled look.

"My English," she said. "I am trying to improve. You said your English is fluent."

"Yes. I went to boarding school in England."

Not knowing what Peter might have told her, he decided to say as little as possible. They moved aside for the remaining men and women to pair up. They were then guided to a larger room for dinner, which included Chinese staples like steamed rice, green beans in black bean sauce, and ma pao tofu, alongside Russian dishes like beef stroganoff and borscht.

The men pulled the chairs for their partners. Alena wobbled in her attempt to sit down. Chen caught her before she stumbled. Her scent, unadorned with fragrance, wafted up his nose, stirring something inside him. He helped her into the chair.

"*Blagodaryu vas,*" she murmured, then switched to Mandarin as if realizing he didn't understand her. "*Xièxiè.*"

He knew a fair amount of Russian and had been tempted to speak with the older woman and a burly, bearded man who both seemed to be from the agency. But if they were involved in anything questionable, he didn't want to come across too prying. Best to start with Alena.

Taking his own seat, he tried not to dwell on how she had felt in his arms. Under different circumstances, he would have been open to bedding her, though the quieter ones usually weren't his type. Given his proclivities when it came to sex, he preferred partners who seemed to have stronger constitutions.

Still, he found himself wondering if someone like Alena could handle any BDSM.

After everyone had sat down, the woman from the agency explained that they would spend four days at the hotel getting to know each other in person and determining if they were right for matrimony. For those who were ready to marry, the agency would arrange for the services on-site.

"Do you wish to marry today or tomorrow?" Alena asked Chen as the others dug into the food.

He tried to hide his surprise. Had Peter offered to marry a woman he had never met in person?

"I don't know," he answered as he poured tea into her porcelain cup and offered to scoop rice onto her plate.

Her lips turned into a small frown. They weren't the plump lips he was used to seeing on women who could afford Botox injections, but they would look pretty enough wrapped around his cock.

Damn. Where did that thought come from? He was here on a mission to find out who had killed Peter and why. Not to get laid.

"You said you could not wait," she said in English.

He thought for a moment before turning the question back on her. "What of you?"

"Me? I like soon."

"But you've only just met me."

"I feel I know you well."

She seemed to try to reassure him with a smile, but her statement was not spoken with a great deal of confidence.

He placed some pelmeni on her plate. "Just because you know someone well doesn't mean you're ready to marry them."

"I am. Ready."

He eyed her more closely. She and Peter had probably gotten to know each other online, via email or some chat room. Peter had clearly not shared his appearance with her. She had to be naive to think she could get to know a person well simply through typing words into a computer. They had no shared experiences.

"You don't know me as well as you think," he said before taking a bite of the chicken. It was mediocre fare, about as good as a lot of the Chinese restaurants in England. "And there are certain elements required for a marriage to be successful."

His father and grandmother had been pestering him of late to marry. As if his sperm might dry up next year. But having suffered the disaster that was his mother and father's marriage, he was in no fucking rush.

She furrowed her brow. "You wrote you love me. Is love not enough?"

Peter had said he loved her? Chen supposed it shouldn't surprise him. Peter fell easily for a pretty face and a sexy body. And Alena, though a tad thin, had both.

"Do you love *me*?" Chen returned.

"Yes," she said and gave him a big smile after a brief pause.

Bullshit. He had heard the hesitation in her response.

"Love isn't enough," he pronounced. "A man and woman must be compatible in temperament and expectations. They must satisfy each other mentally, emotionally...and physically."

The last word seemed to startle her. She must not have given such things much thought. She poked nervously at the food on her plate.

"You should eat," he told her. "Put on some weight."

He didn't know where that last part came from; it wasn't his place or inclination to tell a woman what she should weigh—

except that was what his grandmother was always telling him, and would probably continue to tell him until he weighed three or four hundred pounds.

He had noticed her shoes—which had likely contributed to her clumsiness—were frayed and that her dress, though she looked flush in it, was worn. If she came from a poor background, she should take advantage of the food.

"Is it the money?" she asked, looking at her plate instead of him. "The two million rubles?"

He coughed on his tea. Of course. The little gold digger was marrying Peter for money.

Chen could tolerate stupid women, uncouth women, bitchy women, but he couldn't stand gold diggers. His mother had been the biggest one of all. After swindling tens of millions from his father, she had deserted him, leaving behind a son and daughter, children she obviously cared nothing for.

Chen was tempted to get up in disgust and leave the table. But he had to find out if Alena knew anything that might help solve Peter's murder.

"Like I said, we need to be sure we are compatible."

"How?"

A hunger, not for food, reared inside him. He should have banged one of those nurses making eyes at him back at the hospital. Maybe that would have gotten the desire out of his system.

"Let's start with the physical," he tested her.

Her bottom lip dropped open a tad.

He set down his chopsticks to put his full gaze on her. "My room. Tonight."

CHAPTER 4

All appetite left her, though Alena had been too nervous to eat anyway.

Peter had never spoken about compatibility before. She had been convinced he was head over heels for her. The man sitting beside her, staring at her with cool charcoal eyes—his irises were nearly the same color as his pupils—was not the Peter she had expected.

The women were sharing hotel rooms, five to a room, and there was no rule against staying the night with a man. The men apparently each had their own room, which was not surprising given that they were the ones paying the agency.

She had never actually slept with any of her Chinese husbands before, having managed to leave within hours of being married to them. While, in vastly different circumstances, the thought of sleeping with Peter might have appealed to her, she didn't feel comfortable enough at present.

For certain, she would have felt *safer* with one of the more slender men. Peter, perhaps as a result of a Western diet and life-style, was much more muscular than she had expected to find in a Chinese man.

"Tonight?" she asked, trying to quell the quiver in her voice.

"You said you wanted to be married soon," he returned.

She frowned. He wanted to have sex before they were married? Had she been wrong about Peter? What if he had misled her just so he could have sex? She supposed it would serve her right, as she was being far from honest in her dealings with *him*.

She dared to glance at him. No, a man like him didn't need to go through elaborate schemes to get a woman into his bed.

"You don't look too happy," he observed, his countenance darkening.

"It will be more special after the wedding, no?"

"With you, it will always be special."

That was more what she had expected Peter to say, though a part of her doubted he meant what he said.

She remembered coming across Anna, a Russian woman who had met her Chinese husband through a matchmaking service. Anna had gushed about her marriage, how responsible her husband was, how devoted and kind. The only thing she wished was for her husband to be more romantic. Nevertheless, Alena had envied Anna.

And here she was with the most handsome Asian man she had seen, a man with means, a man who, if she were to believe the stereotypes that led so many Russian women to matchmaking agencies, would be a responsible and devoted husband. Perhaps she should be open to him as a partner?

No. She couldn't officially be married to him because she had never formally divorced her other husbands. Fearful of being prosecuted for what she had done, she had simply disappeared, leaving behind letters with vague explanations that she could not be the sort of wife they deserved.

"Do you not love me?" he inquired, a challenging edge to his tone.

"I-I do," she responded. Worried that her relationship might be in jeopardy, she placed her hand over his. A muscle along his jaw rippled.

"Tonight then," he said, withdrawing his hand.

They finished the dinner in relative silence. Peter was much more brooding than she'd expected, but her mind was more preoccupied with the prospect of having sex with a man she barely knew. She was not at all prepared for this. She didn't have protection on her. Did he? Should she ask one of the other women? Would the hotel have anything?

Or maybe she could get him off so that they wouldn't actually have to couple. Yes. That would be her plan. She would even be willing to go down on him with her mouth if needed. She had heard that usually did the trick with men.

Feeling better, she tried the dessert, a sort of red bean soup. She had not expected to like it as much as she did.

"Have mine," Peter offered when she had finished her bowl.

While she consumed his soup, she felt as if *he* was consuming *her* with his gaze. It made her very uncomfortable, and she was relieved when dinner was over.

Afterward, a number of couples went outside to walk in the gardens in the back of the hotel. A few lingered in the hotel lobby. None appeared to be making their way back to the rooms.

"May I have half an hour?" she asked Peter after he pulled the chair for her. "I have to find someone."

"Half an hour," he replied. "Then meet me in the last room on the fourth floor. Don't keep me waiting too long."

The words could have been spoken out of enthusiasm for what was to come. Instead, they sounded more like a warning to her.

She went in search of George, who always managed to find her. She had saved pieces of fish from the dinner and fed them to her cat. After eating, George purred with contentment in her arms. She decided to bring George with her for moral support.

Her heart skittered as the elevator brought her to the top

floor. She walked down the hall to his room, hugged George closer, and knocked on the door.

Peter opened the door. His gaze fell to the cat.

"This is my cat, George," she introduced.

As if suddenly uncomfortable, George squirmed in her arms.

"Interesting name for a female cat," Peter said.

"Oh, I named her after one of my favorite authors, George Sand, a woman." Noting Peter's grim expression, she asked, "Do you not like cats?"

"No. I don't."

George leaped from her arms and ran down the hall. So much for moral support.

Peter stepped aside for Alena to enter. She noted his room was much larger and nicer than the one she was to share with the other women. His had a balcony that overlooked the gardens and river.

"How lovely," she remarked, walking toward the view.

He went to a sideboard. "Would you like a drink? Kvas? Vodka?"

She rarely drank, but she would need something tonight. "Vodka."

"How do you like it?"

She could not resist a smile. "You have been in the West too long."

He nodded and poured her a shot. She knew that Americans, and perhaps the British as well, liked to mix vodka with other things to form a cocktail, but that diluted the purity of vodka.

She accepted the shot glass from him. "Are you having not any?"

"Not before sex. Especially my kind."

His kind? She assumed he was referring to his ethnicity, though none of the women had ever mentioned any Chinese habits of not drinking before sex. She downed the vodka, then promptly started to cough as the liquid burned her throat.

Peter went quickly to get her water. They exchanged glasses.

"I have not had vodka in many years," she explained after drinking the water. She looked toward the balcony. "May I?"

He opened the balcony doors for her and went to put the glasses away. Outside, she braced herself against the railing and looked out at the last of the light coloring the horizon a dark purple. They were thousands of miles from St. Petersburg, where she had hoped to find a job and settle into some normalcy.

The hairs on her body stood on end, for she felt him behind her. He stood so close she could feel his body heat. She sensed him lowering his head.

"You're nervous," he murmured, his breath a warm breeze on her neck.

She swallowed with difficulty. "It has been...a long time."

She wasn't ready to jump in already. She wanted some conversation first, but she couldn't think of anything to say. His nearness had taken away her ability to think.

He breathed in her scent. She hadn't had the chance to shower upon arriving at the hotel. She wondered if he could smell George on her. She hoped he wasn't allergic to cats. Or maybe it would be good if he started sneezing. Maybe he would skip the sex then.

"Why do you not like cats?" she asked, feeling frozen to the spot, worried that the slightest movement would lead to contact.

"My mother had a cat. It was always hissing and scratching. Caught me near the eye when I was two. Half an inch over and I would have been blind."

"Not all cats are like that. George is—"

The rest of the words were stuck in her throat because he was brushing his knuckles against her upper arm. She hadn't been touched with such sensual gentleness in...forever. And yet her body yearned for more as if it were already addicted.

Alarmed that her body could have such a strong reaction to such a simple caress, she blurted, "I wish for more vodka. Please."

197

He pulled back. "Is that wise? You look like you barely weigh a hundred and ten pounds."

She didn't know what that translated to in terms of grams, but she didn't care. She needed space.

"Please."

He walked back to the sideboard and poured her a shot. She released the breath she had been holding. When he returned, she eagerly accepted the drink from him and relished the burn that went down her throat. He had a glass of water ready as well, but she shook her head, not needing the water this time.

"Drink it," he ordered.

For some reason, she didn't dare disobey. He was probably right to have her drink the water. It wasn't wise to down two shots of vodka given that she hadn't had much for dinner.

He stayed his distance from her this time. She was both relieved and a little disappointed. He crossed his arms and studied her as she took a long sip of the water.

"How is it a beautiful woman like yourself has to resort to a matchmaking service to find a husband?" he asked.

"There are more women than men in Russia," she explained, glad for the conversation. "And it is hard to find a good man. But my friends, they tell me Chinese men make good husbands."

He snorted, a response she found odd. She took another sip of water.

"That's a terrible generalization," he said.

"All women I know who have Chinese husbands are happy."

"What if you're not so lucky?"

Why would he say something like that? she wondered. And how was she supposed to answer that?

"I can't remember," he continued, "if I told you about my preferences where sex is concerned."

She shook her head. He had never mentioned sex in their chats before.

"I suppose I didn't want to scare you."

Did he think Russian women were afraid of sex?

He advanced toward her, and she held up her glass of water to drink as a shield. Standing mere inches from her, he took the glass from her hands and cupped her jaw with his free hand.

"Do you scare easily?"

Why did he ask such a question? Perplexed, she shook her head. His grip on her seemed to tighten a little.

"Good."

Releasing her, he went to replace the glass at the sideboard. He turned around to face her. She wished she could make out his expression. Because his irises were so dark, it was hard to tell if his pupils were dilated or constricted.

With a solemn but commanding tone, he issued his second directive to her. "Strip."

CHAPTER 5

By her quizzical look, he gathered she didn't understand the command.

"Remove the dress," he elucidated.

She stood with her lower lip hanging down, tempting him. He couldn't tell if it was dismay or timidity that stalled her. He was about to inform her that any further delay would incur a punishment, but he didn't want to come on too strongly. Though he shouldn't give a fuck. Like with the vodka. Normally he wouldn't allow a submissive to have more than one drink, especially one who didn't weigh much and hadn't eaten much. But gold diggers deserved whatever hell they made for themselves.

Still, he found he couldn't completely ignore her vulnerability. Which upset him.

"The dress?" she echoed. "Out here?"

"Yes," he replied simply, though he had contemplated offering to rip the dress off her if she didn't take it off herself. When she didn't budge, he added, "I want to see all of you."

She lowered her gaze in thought. Tentatively, she reached behind her back for the zipper. Heat stirred within him as she finally reached to peel the dress down her shoulders. He watched with patience as she paused before gingerly pulling the dress down past her bra. If she wanted to extend the length of her own discomfort, she could take as long as she wanted as far as he was concerned.

The dress continued its descent down her body, slowly exposing her midriff, her hips, her thighs, before finally settling to the floor.

Her chest heaved with uneven breaths. He ran his gaze over every inch of exposed skin. She was rather pale, but that was no surprise. Her white bra and panties were nothing like the fancy lingerie he was accustomed to seeing. Hers were almost adolescent-girl-like in their simplicity. But she looked plenty sexy in them.

He circled her. Her breasts had a nice swell, and she had a decent-sized arse. A little fuller backside would have been better, but women were always beautiful in their nakedness.

He liked what he saw.

He could just take her now. Throw her up against the wall and ravish her without any foreplay. Bend her over the balcony railing and show any passersby what a gold-digging slut she was.

Instead, he brushed her soft brown hair over her shoulders. Her breath quivered.

Noticing a scar above her left hip, he fingered the inch of coarser skin.

"What is this from?"

She hesitated. "I fell down the stairs when I was little."

He trailed his fingers over her abdomen and traced her belly button. "How long has it been since you've had sex?"

"Two, maybe three years."

Damn. She might be as tight as a virgin then.

Leaving his hand on her belly, he stood behind her and pulled her to him. She gave a small gasp. He tucked his fingers slightly into her panties, just below the waistband but not much farther.

"How do you like your sex?" he asked.

She didn't answer for a while. "I do not know."

"You don't know? Have you not had much sex?"

"What quantity is 'much'?"

Maybe she was younger than he'd thought. Or prudish. Though that outfit she wore in the photo Peter had was on the slutty side. Maybe she just didn't have a lot of experience with sex or her number of partners was limited.

"How old are you?"

She seemed surprised, and he realized Peter would probably have known the answer.

"Twenty-three," she answered.

That was a relief. He wouldn't have continued if she was nineteen or younger.

He gently wound his free hand into her hair as his other hand slid lower. He inhaled her scent once more, glad he didn't pick up on any cat smell. He pulled her head to the side, stretching her beautiful swanlike neck. He pressed his lips against her.

Her body tensed and melted against him at the same time. If he were a vampire, he'd go to town on her delectable neck.

"Are you certain you don't know what you like?"

"No. Yes. I do not know," she reiterated.

"You don't know if you like your sex soft and sweet or hard and rough?"

He kissed his way up the side of her neck to her ear.

"Soft and sweet."

Too bad for her. If she weren't a gold digger, he would accommodate her preferences.

"We should go inside," she said softly upon hearing voices below.

The hotel gardens did not extend to the side of the building, were the balcony was, but there was a path that wound from the back of the hotel to the front.

"Not an exhibitionist?" he asked, nudging her ear with his nose. Damn, she smelled good. Though he couldn't describe her actual scent, the blood in his loins churned stronger the more he inhaled.

"No," she confirmed.

Again, too bad. He fit his entire hand in her panties, reaching for her pubis.

She stiffened. "Inside. Please."

Ignoring her plea, he dipped his fingers lower as he asked, "How do you like to come?"

She knit her brows. "Come?"

The voices below grew louder, and she started to wriggle. He tightened his hold on her hair, and she instinctively stopped. She might make a good submissive.

"Don't tell me you've never come during sex," he said, even though he knew many women faked orgasms.

"Maybe. I'm uncertain…"

Uncertain? With him, she would know for damn sure.

"How do you make yourself come?"

"Myself?"

He moved his fingers through her pubic hair and down to her folds. "You masturbate, don't you?"

"Sometimes."

She gasped when he found her clit.

"So you touch yourself."

She whimpered.

He stroked lightly. "Right here?"

"*Da*," she answered.

He fondled her till her clit swelled. The vodka had worked its way into her system, dissolving her earlier resistance. His own arousal pressed hard against his pants. He slid his fingers lower and found her wet. The discovery made his head swim.

He thought again about taking her, without regard to her pleasure. He wondered if Peter would've gotten this far with her. It was Peter she purported to be in love with, but it wasn't Peter she was currently damp for. Technically, she was cheating on

Peter. And though she didn't know that the man touching her wasn't Peter, Chen still felt perturbed on his friend's behalf.

Just fuck her. Use her the way she intends to use Peter.

He was about to do just that—but then he heard her moan, saw her eyelashes flutter and her cheeks blush with arousal.

He wanted to see how she climaxed. Some women experienced small eruptions, others screamed bloody murder. What would Alena be like?

His fingers, now slick with her moisture, glided easily over her clit. He found a spot that made her legs quake. Her arse inadvertently bumped into his crotch. Desire roared in his body, but he kept it at bay long enough for him to send her over the edge.

Despite her concern about being seen by anyone, she cried out—quite loudly. He knew that the sources of the earlier voices were no longer within earshot, having heard the people round the corner, but he doubted she knew that. She trembled forcefully against him, and he thought his hard-on might slice through his pants. He held her through her spasms, till, with a long exhale, she slumped against him.

Sweeping her up into his arms, he carried her inside and tossed her onto the bed.

It was his turn now.

No more Mr. Nice Guy.

Printed in Great Britain
by Amazon